To

with

# Zelda Blair

Love

from

James

x

October 31, 2021

# Zelda Blair

## JANE FOSTER

Charleston, SC
www.PalmettoPublishing.com

*Zelda Blair*

First Edition

Hardcover ISBN: 978-1-63837-358-2
Paperback ISBN: 978-1-63837-357-5
eBook ISBN: 978-1-63837-356-8

I would like to acknowledge these amazingly helpful people who spent hours of their time helping me create *Zelda Blair*:

Donna Miller Casey
Mary Jean Gulden
Sally Johnson
Dr. Mary Zachary-Caginard
and all the members of Paris Creative Writers,
especially Grahame Elliot

Thank you from the bottom of my heart.

This book is dedicated to my dearly beloved family
zoomers without whom I would not have survived lockdown

# Contents

# Chapter One

Zelda Blair looked up at the steep hill and shook her head. No way.

Phoebe and Chloe, aged three and five, were hanging on to her hands, hopping, whining, squirming with all their might. Above them the fog-cloaked San Francisco sky loomed blank and inscrutable.

At least it isn't raining, Zelda thought, but she could tell her shoes were dead set against her. Sensational gladiator platforms though they were, the chances of getting home with them still on her feet were not good.

Zelda bent down and tried to unfurl from the girls. Their hands were sticky. Now her long, tapered fingers were sticky, too, and she hesitated to touch the shoes for fear of spoiling the expensive lavender leather. Regrettably, the angle of the hill was in cahoots with the Christian Louboutins. She toppled over.

Phoebe and Chloe howled in their chocolate-stained party dresses. Zelda paused, lying still on the sidewalk for a moment, focusing on the vibration their screams created. It was the perfect audio for her present mood. She felt defeated and needy, but giving up was not an option. She'd never consider such a thing.

"Come on, kids. Last one home's a rotten egg."

With Zelda hobbled by her fashion choice, the race to the top of the hill was suitably handicapped. The two little girls arrived at the front door of the big brick house an instant before their mother, winded and laughing.

"And the well-shod blondes win by a nose," Zelda announced.

Everyone wanted to know the Blairs. They were everything everyone wanted to be. Good looking, slender, smart, athletic and if not actually rich, at least they appeared to be rich, and certainly they had plans to become rich. Didn't Nick work diligently at Silverman? And wasn't Zelda one of the best hostesses of the thirty-something set in San Francisco's Pacific Heights?

The Blairs were invited everywhere, and they went. They went to the Opera and the Winter Ball in black tie. They went to Strictly Bluegrass and Zoofest in blue jeans. They even had hopes of being invited to join the junior council of the Museum of Modern Art. It was not a stretch anymore now that Nick was making such fecund donations.

But most of all, Nick and Zelda hoped to host school fundraisers in their house at the top of Pierce Street. They hoped to host them for Burke's and Town when their children were old enough to attend these elite bastions of primary education. This was a hope shared by both husband and wife, if for different reasons.

Still laughing, Zelda and the girls stumbled through the marble entrance hall and headed towards the back of the house. In the enormous kitchen, Lourdes, the nanny, sat on the canvas-covered sofa sewing a button on a tiny blue cardigan. She was a plump but fit woman of about fifty, immaculate and efficient. Despite her age, there was not a sign of gray in her short dark hair.

"Matt and Miles have just settled down," she said. "I know it's early, but Matt was fussy. Let me get the girls into a bath before supper." Matt and Miles were good-natured year-old twins.

"No bath!" the girls protested. "We want to watch Peppa Pig."

Firmly, but kindly, Zelda said, "Lourdes is in charge here, and if I hear any complaints there'll be no dessert tonight, and no Peppa Pig for a week." That was that, and the tired little blonde girls and their weary mommy went to their separate tubs and bathed in bubbles.

Some of Zelda's acquaintances privately thought she was too strict with her children but never dared voice an opinion. Zelda didn't ask them what they thought and didn't care. This was how she'd been brought up, and this was how she would bring up her four. She'd been one of eight and had watched her own mother run a seamless household and raise her green-eyed brood with grace and dignity on much less money than Zelda had at her disposal. Zelda would do it her way. She had to acknowledge it wasn't all bad that Nick was never around.

Zelda stretched out in the soothing water and looked down at the bruises strewn across her abdomen. She was not going to dwell on them now and propelled her mind back to happier times. She soaked, thinking about her father who'd risen in the ranks of the NYPD and was now the police commissioner of New York City. As a kid, she'd always been afraid a bad guy would get him and that he'd never come home again to toss her in the air. He was kind, smart and self-disciplined. For her, he was the model of what all men should be.

Her mother, on the other hand, loved literature and for the past twelve years had been a full professor of American Lit at Adelphi University in Garden City. Bless them, her parents, still lived in the same house in Bayside, Queens, and still attended Mass every Sunday at St. Francis de Sales.

It was her mother who'd decided that all her children would be named after famous writers. Zelda Fitzgerald O'Neill Blair was the youngest sister of William Faulkner O'Neill, Eugene no-middle-name O'Neil, Edith Wharton O'Neill, Emily Dickenson O'Neill, Mark Twain O'Neill, Dorothy Parker O'Neill and Henry James O'Neill. How *could* her father have let her do it to them? Zelda often wondered, but she loved all of them, each and every one, the parents, the siblings and the literary giants for whom they were named. As for her own children, she preferred names based on how they sounded to her musical ear.

Zelda slipped lower into the scented steam and thought back. Of course, the O'Neil kids never mentioned their middle names. And no one ever asked, either. It was Billy, Gene, Edie, Em, Mark, Dot and Hank. And then, there was Zelda. Hard then. Cool now, even the Fitzgerald part. None of the others had fallen very far from the family tree, having chosen careers in criminal justice and education. And then, there was Zelda. All of the others religiously paid into 401Ks, and then there was Zelda.

From where she lay in the marble bath she could see the luxurious Porthault towels hanging in profusion from Lucite bars. The mirrored doors leading to her dressing room stood ajar reminding her how different her wardrobe was to her siblings', how different it was living here at the top of the hill.

Grander, she thought, but not necessarily better. How odd. She'd always assumed marrying Nick and living in this huge house thousands of miles away from his disapproving mother would ensure her happiness, and yet it was here that it all had started. Not really violence, she thought, just surprising and painful moments. At first she thought it was an aberration related to work stress. But then the bruises continued to appear, dark and angry on her torso. They always vanished before another episode occurred. She'd be safe for a while.

Four days ago she'd installed white noise machines in the children's bedrooms. If she turned them on at night, turned them off again in the morning and got into that habit, she figured the children would never hear. The muscles in her abdomen tightened instinctively at the thought of what they shouldn't hear. She consciously released them, giving a little spread to her shoulders as the osteopath had suggested. Of course, she might be overreacting. Nick didn't like her to overreact, but he hadn't berated her for getting the machines, she'd noticed.

Zelda felt refreshed after her bath, and by the time Nick came home she was preparing for the evening ahead. From the bedroom window, where she stood massaging cream into her cuticles, she could see his lanky frame bouncing up the flagstone path, taking the steps two at a time. She noticed the wisteria was beginning to bloom. Soon the red brick would be covered in fragrant lilac blossoms.

Her clothes were neatly laid out in the dressing room, and she was looking for the right evening bag when she heard Nick at the door. She wished he'd remove his shoes before stepping on the thick, cream-colored wool carpet, but he never did. He regarded housekeeping concerns beneath him but would gladly have the room re-carpeted monthly if that's what it took. Masters of the Universe didn't pad around in stocking feet. What was the matter with Zelda that she didn't know a universal truth like that?

"Tonight let's ditch the kids and go out to celebrate. Today was the final match. You're looking at the kickboxing champion of the Pacific Rim," Nick bragged, posing in front of a wall of mirrors. At thirty-seven, his bushy blond hair was beginning to show signs of gray at the temples, only making him more attractive to Zelda.

"Way to go, champ," Zelda managed. "But it's Brooke's fortieth, don't forget, and the party's at Battery."

"Oh, right. I'll jump in the shower." Nick never wanted an evening at home. It had always been like that.

Zelda sat on the edge of the bed and concentrated on applying clear polish to her short, but no longer bitten, nails. Brooke will distract him tonight, she thought, but not knowing how she felt about that.

Sometimes Zelda considered Brooke one of her best friends. Both their husbands worked at Silverman, one of the largest international investment banks. They'd met at the company party welcoming the Blairs to San Francisco six years before. Brooke was seven years older than Zelda, brunette and glamorous as well as savvy in West Coast ways. At first she looked askance at this New York interloper, but once she'd discovered Zelda was a fount of knowledge on the subject of American Literature, she invited Zelda to join the book club. It was an exclusive group of intellectually pretentious young women married to financial and tech wunderkinds or scions of San Francisco's high society. No outsiders were ever included.

Brooke took Zelda under her wing in other ways, too, and made sure she displayed all the right brands, from Federic Fekkai tresses to Chanel polished toes. The right brands included not only clothes and cosmetics, but extended to interior designers, doctors, insurance companies, restaurants, vacation destinations and employment agencies as well. Nothing was left to chance for the Silverman wife. The aim was perfection. They all knew this, but Zelda had not been compliant until Brooke took charge. Brooke was the arbiter of elegance in this regard, but it was probably due to her husband's senior position in the company rather than to Brooke's innate good taste.

Stanford valedictorian Donna Hall was the founder and leading light of the book club. Brooke's first personal coup in this arena was proposing Zelda for membership. With Zelda being the well-read daughter of an American Literature professor, Brooke had seen Donna and raised her one.

For Brooke, the best part of it all was seeing patrician Donna meet her match. She loved seeing how flustered Donna had become in giving literary critiques when Zelda was in attendance. Zelda instinctively understood that Donna was her intellectual superior in every subject other than American Lit, but Donna's opinions at the book club, which had once been delivered with laser-like certainty, now scuttled out like apologies. Brooke took note of this, looked down at her dazzling twelve-carat diamond ring and smiled. Slowly the power over the book club women was shifting in Brooke's favor.

The subtleties of this takeover had not been lost on Zelda. She knew Brooke was ambitious and admired her for it. Brooke always knew what she wanted and how to get it. Zelda was less than enthusiastic about some of her tactics, but she understood. There was pressure at home. For Silverman wives, there was always pressure at home.

Brooke's husband, Stuart Duncan, was a robust man with curly brown hair and piercing blue eyes. He was the head of Nick's division at Silverman, and as a prodigious producer, he commanded great respect. A driven man, ravenous for success in every corner of his life, Stuart demanded excellence from himself and everyone else. Anyone not up to snuff would soon hear about it. He was known to be harsh, but he rewarded brilliance and loyalty, at home, at work, at play.

As she waited for her nails to dry, Zelda inspected her face in the mirror. Irish genes were strong, showing in her clear pale skin, which complimented her green eyes and dark red hair. In these aspects she closely resembled her siblings, but her features were more chiseled, and she towered-over her sisters. At 5' 10", she was nearly as tall as her father and brothers.

Staring into the mirror, she fiddled with her bangs, always self-conscious that her forehead might be considered too high for her heart-shaped face.

It was going to be a spectacular party, she told herself. No expense would be spared. It had to be a triumph.

# Chapter Two

And a triumph it was. Brooke had managed to keep the theme secret, and even Zelda was shocked to see her standing at the entrance of Battery greeting her two hundred guests in a classic circus ringmaster costume, complete with shiny black boots and whip. A red feather boa was wrapped around her throat. Brooke was a Taurus who regularly consulted her astrologer, and according to all sources, red around the neck was required for extracting the best out of her planets. Tonight she looked both magnificent and menacing.

All the rooms were tented in turquoise. Mixed in with the wait staff were masked acrobats who wore leopard-spotted leotards, and three of them paraded cheetahs on leashes.

Spontaneous performances occurred throughout the evening, but the only spotlight shone on Sonny Rollins when he joined the band to blow his sax-y version of Happy Birthday. Brooke had arranged for her husband's saxophone to be on stage next to the legend, and Stuart's outlandish dream of performing with Sonny came true.

"All it takes is money, honey, but then you already knew that," Nick whispered into Zelda's diamond earring. "And this is supposed to be Brooke's birthday, not Stuart's. So why are we being subjugated to this cacophonous sludge?"

"You tell me," Zelda purred.

"Because Brooke's smart as well as beautiful. Brooke never forgets who brings home the bacon." Nick gave his wife a hard look.

Zelda ignored him and scanned the room looking for Donna Hall. Not seeing her, she picked up her evening bag and set off to find her.

Donna was the rare jewel who didn't require a setting. Zelda had to search her out and marveled at how Donna always managed to be elusive, looking both dignified and sexy while sounding brilliant and modest. Donna put the *b* into *subtle,* and Zelda wondered if she could ever figure out how to befriend this paragon without alienating Brooke.

Spotting her quarry, Zelda zoomed in. Donna was laughing with her dinner partner, her thick blond hair waving back from her classically beautiful face. Zelda hesitated. She listened intently, hovering close to the table, but finally decided against interrupting the conversation. Threading her way through the crowded room to her own table, she noticed Brooke sitting in her place, flirting with her husband. For a brief moment she felt adrift, but that was quickly washed away by a wave of relief. She was free to cruise the room on her own, now free from the obligation to perform in any way.

The band left the makeshift stage, and the music was turned over to a DJ from LA, a sure sign that Sonny and Stuart's gig was up. Zelda was minding her own business, leaning against a wall watching acrobatic feats a few yards away. Without warning, Stuart's steel grip encircled her waist, the line of his mouth stern. "My wife's busy hitting on your husband, and I'm horny as hell. Let's get out of here." His voice was soft and full of malevolence.

Zelda looked at him in mock disbelief. Although her Catholic school training hadn't prepared her for men like Stuart, experience had. This was not the first time she'd had unsolicited attention from a man whom she'd dared not offend. Stuart was confident. Too handsome, too smooth. Too sure of himself. Zelda found him repulsive.

"You flatter me, Stuart, but you need to save that kind of sweet talk for the birthday girl." She slowly turned away and glided from the wall to the center of the tented room.

The party rocked on well into Saturday morning, but Zelda never managed to corner Donna. The music was ear-splittingly loud and Donna was often dancing, so after several attempts, Zelda went back to her table and found her place next to Nick was empty. She pulled him onto the dance floor, realizing that any conversation with Donna tonight would be nothing more than shouted inanities. Yet again, this was neither the time nor the place.

Sacrosanct Saturday morning family breakfasts had slowly slipped away. Nick could no longer be counted on. Golf with a client or colleague, kickboxing competitions or even 'catching up on things' at the office took precedence, and Zelda frequently presided alone.

The morning after the party, Zelda was in her kitchen dishing out banana pancakes to the kids when Brooke appeared with her teenaged daughters.

"Taylor and Audrey will look after the kids. You and I have a party post-mortem to do."

Phoebe and Chloe danced around the older girls, and the twins banged their spoons on the highchair trays in delight.

Zelda gave Taylor and Audrey a squeeze. "You girls are very popular around here. If there are any questions, Lourdes has all the answers."

"Let me grab a cup of coffee and let's go up to your room." Brooke seemed no worse for wear despite the late night.

Zelda took off her apron and handed it to Lourdes. "Try to keep a lid on it, and I'll be back."

"Everything's under control here, Mrs. Blair. Don't you worry."

"Love hearing you say that, Lourdes."

The two women went upstairs and sat on Zelda's canopied bed. "That was the best party this town has seen, ever. How did you keep the secret?"

"The only way to keep a secret is to tell no one, and I promised the staff at Battery there would be bonuses if no one breathed a word. Stuart gawked when he saw how I was dressed. He had no idea and about fainted when Sonny Rollins called him to the stage."

"You're the bomb, Brooke. No one else could've pulled it off. Did your girls come? I didn't see them."

"They were there through the Sonny Rollins thing. Then they took off. Friday night when you're fifteen and thirteen is more fun anywhere other than your mother's birthday party."

"That was some party."

"It was great, but we have other things to talk about."

"I thought this was the post-mortem."

"I hate post-mortems. I have news. Donna asked me to chair the book club next season. I want to kill it and need your suggestions."

"My mother occasionally gives herself a break from American Lit and goes on a Jane Austen bender. We could do all six of her classics. What do you think?"

"Good idea. Do you know any literary scholars who'd come and talk to us?"

"No, but Mom would certainly have some good recommendations."

Brooke rubbed her hands together. "A Jane Austen bender. That's what we need. Get on to your mother, will you? I want to have the world's best speaker signed up right away."

"I'll call her now."

According to Zelda's mother, Dr. Abigail O'Neil, Stanford English Professor Grace Lloyd was considered one of the great Jane Austen scholars, and although Dr. O'Neil had never met

Dr. Lloyd, she'd read her book on the Janeites, an enthusiastic group of Austen fans. She told her daughter she'd found the book both incisive and amusing, much like Miss Austen herself.

By the time Brooke left with Taylor and Audrey, she'd convinced Zelda to make a call to the professor first thing on Monday morning.

It was surprisingly easy to reach Dr. Lloyd who listened patiently as Zelda introduced herself, recited the relevant details and said, "We would like you to speak at our opening meeting in early October as well as at the closing one in late May."

Zelda was pleased when Dr. Lloyd agreed and added, "There will be a handsome honorarium for you."

"An honorarium won't be necessary, dearie, but you should know, I don't give traditional lectures. What I'll do for you is a round table discussion. Early October's good for me. I'll bring a couple of my doctoral candidates, and we'll discuss whatever we happen to be working on at the time. Nothing prepared, you understand, and we'll do all the talking."

"That sounds great."

"By the way, I read the paper your mother published on Dorothy Parker. I howled. She's a very funny woman, your mother."

"She named all her children after American writers. I have a Dorothy Parker sister."

"You must be Zelda Fitzgerald, then."

"Indeed, I am."

"Far out."

Zelda hoped her laugh wasn't audible. She couldn't wait to meet Dr. Lloyd. "We'll set a date, and then, may I bring a written confirmation to your office?"

"Listen, dearie, I am, as Dorothy Parker said, 'Too fucking busy, and vice versa.' Call me after Labor Day and give me the date." And with that she hung up.

Delighted to have scored such an eccentric, Zelda called Brooke with the news. "It'll be totally different. In your living room, we can put armchairs around the fireplace for Dr. Lloyd *et al*, and then make two rows of ten with a middle aisle. There's plenty of room."

"I don't know. She sounds kind of whacky. Are you sure about this? I've got to *crush* it."

"You will. Trust me."

"How do we know her students will be any good?"

"Come on, Brooke, they're PhD candidates at Stanford. Anyone can get a lecturer – this will be much cooler."

"I suppose you're right. What's the name of her book again?"

"I forget. Google it."

"Better yet, I'll read it. Can you make sure they'll stay for lunch? I want this to be the most interesting opening meeting ever. And I'll make the luncheon unforgettable. Donna may regret giving the chair to me, and she'd better watch out, I may never give it back."

Zelda switched the subject. "What are you planning for summer?"

"I'm taking Taylor and Audrey to a dude ranch in the Grand Tetons for three weeks. I've already started feeling sorry for my poor thighs. God, I hate being saddle sore."

"Is Stuart going with you?"

"You know Stuart Duncan never gives it a rest. He'll come for a weekend or two. What about you?"

"Going to Disneyland with Phoebe and Chloe. The twins are too young and Nick's too busy working for Stuart. I wish we had book club all year round."

"Other people have lives and actually leave San Francisco." Brooke sounded distracted. "When are you going to Disney?"

"End of June. I'm driving. It's a bitch of a drive, but I want to have my car down there."

"Hope you're staying at the Disneyland Hotel."

"Of course."

"What did you say your dates are again?"

"I didn't say."

"So what are they?"

"I'd have to look at my calendar. June twenty-something to June twenty-something plus three."

"Let me know. Maybe you'd like to take Taylor and Audrey as your assistants."

"Oh my God! We'd all love that. I'll check and text you."

# Chapter Three

Taylor and Audrey were a godsend during the drive from San Francisco to Anaheim. They sang, played games and napped with Phoebe and Chloe in back of Zelda's blue Tesla SUV for the seven-hour trip.

Mickey and Minnie Mouse were at the entrance of the hotel to greet them and show them around the pirate cove-themed pool area and Goofy's kitchen before taking them to their suite. Both bedrooms had two queen-sized beds, and there was a large but sparsely furnished living room in between. Zelda staked out one room with her two, and the Duncan girls took the other. They split to bathe and change for supper.

After their baths, the four girls sat around drinking Cokes and playing Go Fish in the living room while waiting for Zelda to finish dressing. Drawing a new card, Phoebe upturned her glass and needed a change of clothes. Taylor took charge and opened the door of the Blair bedroom.

Zelda was standing naked, facing the door, a bath towel lying on the bed in front of her. Instinctively, she grabbed the towel, covered the front of her body and turned sideways.

Taylor gasped. "Mrs. Blair, what happened to you?" Her eyes were wide, emphasizing the blueness of her stare.

Zelda looked down at her exposed skin and saw the large, livid bruise through Taylor's eyes.

"Oh, it's a birthmark. And didn't your darling mother tell you never, ever, ever open a door without knocking?" Zelda tried to sound lighthearted and non-judgmental, but cursed Brooke for her lax parenting style.

"I'm so sorry. I didn't mean to walk in on you, but Phoebe spilled her Coke and needs something dry to wear.

"I'll bring something out in a minute."

Zelda wrapped herself in the hotel's terry cloth robe and a big smile. With a small yellow sundress in hand, she went to the living room and chatted casually while Phoebe changed clothes.

At Trader Sam's Enchanted Tiki Bar, they had Polynesian Punch and Spring Rolls for supper, and although there was a lot of joking at the table, Taylor seemed quieter than usual. Zelda felt uneasy and wondered if she suspected.

Over the last few years, Zelda had become fond of the Duncan girls. Taylor was the image of her mother, tall with long dark hair and china blue eyes. But she had none of her mother's scheming ways and was genuinely kind and thoughtful of others. Shy and young for her age, but clearly destined to become a great beauty, Taylor had the gangly look of a colt.

Audrey, on the other hand, was a boisterous prankster, with freckles and an impressive set of braces on her teeth. She hadn't had her growth spurt, so her hands and feet looked too big for her small dense body. An Honor Roll student with an extensive vocabulary, Audrey could make anyone laugh, but Zelda intuited some calculation behind the humor. This apple definitely didn't fall very far from the tree, Zelda thought, or as her Irish grandmother would say, she didn't lick it from the stones in the road.

The next day at lunch in The Blue Bayou restaurant, Phoebe said, "What's a birthmark, Mom?"

Taylor looked at Zelda with alarm and apology in her eyes.

18

Ignoring Taylor, Zelda tousled Phoebe's hair. "It's a mark on your skin that some people have when they're born."

"Do I have one? Does Chloe?"

"No, and neither do Matt or Miles. Now, who's going to have dessert? I see they have mile high ice-cream pie. That's what I'm going for."

Later in the afternoon, Zelda put her arm around Taylor's shoulders and pulled her aside. "Don't worry, honey. Birthmarks are rare, and it's weird when you see one for the first time. Do me a favor, though, and don't mention it to your mom."

"I'm sorry, Mrs. Blair. Does it hurt? It looks like it hurts."

"Not at all. Forget about it."

Two days later as they were loading the car for the long haul back to San Francisco, little Chloe rammed into her mother's side. Zelda winced and noticed Taylor staring at her.

"Goodness, Chloe, you're like a Mack truck. Watch out or you'll make big dents in cars and tanks and people!" Zelda bent down and kissed Chloe on the top of her head. She straightened and continued as if nothing had happened.

All was quiet in the car when Brooke's call came through. "I've got everything under control for the luncheon. Liane says my stars on Wednesday, October second are perfect for hosting a party."

"I can't believe you're on it already."

"Wait 'til you hear. Stanlee Gatti is on board to do the party planning, and we're going to have the wait staff dressed in full Regency rig. A pianoforte and harp will be delivered on September thirtieth and on the first the musicians will come to practice."

"I can't believe this. Where on earth are you going to put them all?"

"I'm sending everything in the entrance hall to storage. Stanlee says there's plenty of room, and we'll have a flute and violin as well, everyone in period dress playing Regency songs and ballads. Jane Austen's favorites, of course. And a Jane Austen menu, too. McCall's is going to buy cookbooks on the subject and make it authentic."

"I can't believe you're consulting *Stanlee* for a book club meeting. Don't you think that's a bit much?"

"No. And I've already had Patrick come over from Bloomers to give me his suggestions. He's going to look up what could've been blooming in Jane's garden in early October and try to stick to that. Isn't it the best?"

"I hope Stuart won't mind footing the bill."

"Are you kidding? It'll be written up in *The Nob Hill Gazette*, etc. He'll be thrilled."

"Donna won't like it if you invite the press." Zelda put on her blinker and changed lanes.

"I won't invite them, then. Someone will leak it. Don't worry, she'll never know it was me."

"Weren't you the one who said the secret of keeping a secret is to tell no one?"

"This time I want people to know. Donna's rule of never posting anything on social media would mean no one would ever see. This is expensive. Far too expensive for twenty book club members."

"You're a force of nature, Brooke. Like extreme weather or something."

"I take it you approve."

"I wouldn't miss it for the world."

That evening, back home in San Francisco, with the kids down for the night, Zelda and Nick were eating spaghetti in the kitchen.

"I think Brooke is making some kind of social gaffe," Zelda said.

"Brooke doesn't make gaffes."

"Listen to this. She's got the same team doing a *book club* meeting at her house as she had for her fortieth. McCall's is doing Nineteenth Century food and serving it in period costume. For only twenty people."

"Since when do you need to have a lot of people to do something outstanding?"

"Since *forever*." Where she came from, extravagances like this were frowned upon, maybe because the frowners were envious, but she thought Nick would find it vulgar.

"It sounds inspired to me," Nick said. "And Brooke knows how to make things memorable. Stuart likes Brooke to put on a big show. And what would you know about social gaffes, anyway?"

Zelda was silent, thinking back on all the times comments like this had hurt her. She didn't feel hurt this time but wondered why Nick was defending Brooke and what might have happened while she was away.

This thought kept running around in her mind, disturbing her sleep. Finally at 3:30 a.m., she got out of bed and went to the kitchen. While she heated water for tea, she texted her mother, "If you're up, call my cell." It was early morning in New York.

Moments later she picked up the vibrating phone. Abigail O'Neil's voice was strong and clear. "What are you doing up so late?"

"Mom, remember when I wanted to be a flight attendant? I keep mulling over what that life would have been like."

"Zelda, what are you doing thinking such thoughts in the middle of the night?"

"Just considering those exotic ports of call. I haven't left California since we arrived here six years ago."

"You've had four children. Much better than all the exotic ports in the world."

"You're right, but still..."

"What is it, my darling?"

"Nothing specific. I'm feeling homesick. I want to come soon and bring the kids."

"This house could use some kids. Come this summer. Dad and I would love it. The little ones would have a blast with all their cousins. And I'd have a chance to interrogate you."

"Interrogate me?"

"The three times I've been out there has been all about babies, and you never give a sense of what's really going on when we speak on the phone."

"I call you practically everyday."

"And you talk about the children and what you're doing, but nothing about what you are feeling or thinking."

"I don't have time to feel or think."

"Come home then. I'll take care of the children, and you can sit around feeling and thinking."

"You're on, Mom. I'll talk to Nick this morning."

"Even if Nick can't come, you come with the kids."

Not a problem there, Zelda thought. Nick won't care when we go or how long we stay as long as I dress the children in matching clothes and go visit his mother who'll make sure the moment is captured by a famous photographer.

# Chapter Four

At 5 a.m. when Nick came down for breakfast, Zelda was still in the kitchen. "I'd like to take the kids East this summer for a few weeks," she said. "Can you get away at all?"

"I can't. You know that. But please don't go."

"I haven't been home in six years. I'm always either pregnant or postpartum, and I really want to spend some time with my parents."

"Why don't they come out here? It would be great to have them here."

"No, Nick, I need a real O'Neil fix. I have lots of nieces and nephews whom I've only met on Skype. What kind of aunt is that?"

Nick frowned, and Zelda tensed.

"Well, okay, but leave the twins and Lourdes here. You go with the girls. I'd be too lonely if all of you went. We guys had a great time while you were at Disneyland."

"You never cease to amaze me."

"What man doesn't like time alone with his sons? We'll eat ice-cream and go to the zoo."

As soon as Nick left for work, Zelda called her mother. "The girls and I are coming. I can't tell you how surprised I am, but Nick wants to keep the boys here. Usually he doesn't notice the kids at all."

"He doesn't want to rattle around in that big house all by himself."

"Or maybe he wants them as protection from predators."

"Don't tell me you have troubles on that front."

Zelda paused before answering, "I'm not sure."

"Maybe you shouldn't leave town."

"I feel conflicted. You know I'm crazy about Nick, but sometimes he seems detached. And then he shows me his adorable side, like this morning. I'm deeply touched that he wants to have the twins stay with him. It makes me want to stay right here and never leave. But I'm homesick for you and Dad, too."

"Well, you're always welcome here. Think it over, and let me know." Zelda heard her mother sigh before the phone went dead.

Zelda checked Brooke's dates in Wyoming and decided on twelve days on Long Island in late July while Brooke was far away. She booked a flight for herself and the girls, leaving on a Monday, coming back on the Friday of the following week, ensuring Nick had only one weekend alone.

On the morning of July fourth, Zelda was brushing her teeth and saw Nick in the mirror moving towards her. She leaned over to rinse her mouth and didn't see the vicious leg thrust come at her. She'd always seen it before and tightened her abs, deflecting the blow somewhat. This time the force of the kick threw her body towards the mirror. It was the depth of the sink that saved her from a severe blow to the head. Shockwaves skittered through her, but her first thought was, I should have tensed my muscles, followed quickly by, I'll need a one-piece bathing suit. As the pain began to register, she knew this one would result in more than just bruised ribs.

Nick was moody for the rest of the day and did not join in on the picnic Zelda had planned across the street at Alta Plaza Park. Lovemaking that night was gentle, and Zelda wondered if she should tell her mother about this pattern.

The following day there was blood in her urine. A Google search suggested a bruised kidney. That didn't sound too bad.

By the eighteenth of July, there was no more blood, and she and the girls left for New York on the red-eye. Kevin and Abigail O'Neil were at Kennedy airport to meet them, and Phoebe and Chloe tumbled into their outstretched arms with Zelda stumbling along after, beaming sleepily at the sight of her girls enveloped by her parents.

Kevin O'Neil stood six foot one and his solidity made him appear even larger. His authority over his children had been absolute and irreversible. Growing up under his protection had given Zelda a feeling of security, almost a sense of being invulnerable.

On the drive home, Abigail twisted her agile frame to face the back seat. She wore pearl earrings, which Zelda hadn't seen before, and Zelda thought, maybe this is how I'll look in thirty years, grey-streaked auburn hair with fans of wrinkles framing my eyes and pearls on my ears. She smiled at her mother and thought how calm and dignified she looked, like a fount of wisdom.

"When we get to the house, I'll bathe the girls in your old bathroom, and you can stretch out in my tub. I think you'll approve of the changes I've made."

"Don't worry, Mom. Nothing wrong with me that a gallon of coffee won't cure."

"Let me brew a pot and put it by the tub before I leave for the office," Kevin said. Zelda felt her neck muscles relax. There was safety in the sound of his voice. It wouldn't really matter what he said, the low even tones were a healing balm to her strained muscles.

"No, Dad. I'll drink coffee with you in the kitchen until you leave for work, and then I'll take Mom up on her offer. I can't tell you how long I've wanted to have her bathtub all to myself. I'm not sharing it with a pot of coffee."

As they pulled up to the three-story weathered shingle house, Zelda jumped out and opened her arms wide, "Hello, house! I'm so glad to see you."

"Mom, the house can't hear you." Phoebe rolled her eyes in her grandmother's direction.

"Yes, of course it can. Don't you be so silly. This house loves me and wants to hear my news."

"You're the silly one, Mommy." Chloe said.

"Come on in, girls, and see if you can tell which bedroom was your mother's when she was your age." Abigail would make sure they chose the right one. "Most of your aunts and uncles and cousins are coming for supper tonight. After your bath, you can explore, but there'll be naps after lunch so you can stay up late."

"I know everyone already from their pictures and Skype," Chloe said proudly.

"Me, too. And Uncle Hank came to San Francisco when I was little," said five-year-old Phoebe.

Once inside, Zelda marveled. How on earth did we all fit in here? It had been so much bigger in her mind, but the house still had the happy vibe she knew from childhood.

By ten, Zelda was floating in soapy water surveying the scene. The Formica counter had been replaced by marble, the shiny silver wallpaper had disappeared in favor of high gloss apricot paint and the shower curtain matched the wall color. Jean Naté products were neatly lined up by height on the rim of the tub alongside a battery operated scrubbing brush with a long plastic handle. Pristine white towels were rolled in a basket. Prefect order reigned. Alas, the enamel was thinning around the drain leaving streaky black marks.

Reading her surroundings, Zelda accepted that she couldn't lay her troubles here in this innocent place. Tears flowed freely from her eyes. I'm exhausted, she thought. The flight.

As she toweled off, she stared sadly at the yellowing bruises. They would have to remain her secret.

For lunch with Nick's mother, Phoebe and Chloe wore white dresses embroidered with cherries and trimmed in red. Abigail took dozens of pictures with her old Nikon before waving good-bye to them as they sped off in a black Uber SUV.

The real Mrs. Blair, for that is how Zelda thought of her, lived on the east side of Park Avenue between Eighty-first and Eighty-second Streets in a pre-war building with a clean limestone façade and white-glove service. Despite the stately serenity of the old edifice, Zelda felt anxious and fussed over the girls' hair in the elevator. A sizzle of nervousness passed through her like an electric shock as she pressed the doorbell of apartment Eleven A.

Napoleon opened the door right away as if he had been waiting for the ring. He'd been Marion Blair's chef for many years before Zelda came on the scene.

"Napoleon, how lovely to see you. Meet Phoebe and Chloe!"

The old man's kind face was wreathed in smiles as he hugged the girls and wrung Zelda's hand before showing them into the living room. Marion was seated in her habitual spot on the chintz sofa near the fireplace. Negative energy was ubiquitous as if it were seeping out through the wiring.

"Come, come, girls, and give your old Granny a kiss. Napoleon, please bring me a gin martini. Shirley Temples for the girls. And what about you, Zelda?'

Zelda knew her mother-in-law would like her to join in with a martini, but delighting in being reckless, she said, "A ginger ale, please," and felt a silent dart of disapproval pass her way.

Marion Blair always amazed Zelda with how easily she talked to children when it suited her. Always meticulously groomed and very dressed-up, she looked like the kind of person who would not encourage affection from the young, but like her son, she had the ability to surprise. As the girls were getting a double dose of their grandmother's charm, Zelda's eyes swept the large, formal room.

She could not help noticing paint peeling in several spots, and the lovely old Aubusson rug looked threadbare and in need of a good clean. Now that she thought about it, why was Napoleon answering the door? Where was Francesca? Francesca, who'd always run the house with an iron hand.

As if reading her mind, Marion said, "Napoleon went home to the Philippines for a month. He just returned last week. And Francesca retired in January. There's no such thing as replacing Francesca, so I didn't even try. Anyway, I don't entertain so much any more."

"Everything looks as lovely as ever. I'm sorry about Francesca. You must miss her terribly."

"I do. She moved back to Portugal. We talk on the phone every Sunday."

Zelda could see the sadness in the older woman's eyes and was on the verge of feeling sorry for her when the martini arrived. Within ten minutes Marion was back to being the bitch Zelda had come to dread, restrained barbs flying through the air like so many invisible arrows. Her disapproval of Zelda in particular and current affairs in general was as thinly veiled as possible, smudging the atmosphere with bitterness.

Twenty minutes later luncheon was served in the dining room. The mahogany table was shining and the linen placemats and napkins were snowy white, but the silver was not freshly polished, and the curtains looked deflated, as if the stuffing had been knocked out of them. Even the dahlias in the bud vases looked like they'd seen better days.

Marion had a small glass of red wine with the cheese soufflé and a flute of Champagne with the plum pie. After lunch they went to the walnut-paneled library, and Daisy, Marion's eleven-year-old English cocker spaniel came waddling into the room. One of her eyes was hazy with a cataract, but a blue satin bow perched on each ear proclaimed she was freshly groomed. Daisy greeted the girls with enthusiasm and then sat quietly at Marion's side.

As Napoleon poured steaming coffee into delicate demi- tasse cups, Marion said to him, "Please get your phone so you can take some pictures of the girls with Daisy. Phoebe and Chloe look so sweet in their cherry dresses."

Napoleon got snapping. Excited by all the attention, Daisy pawed her mistress's ankles making runs in her stockings. Marion's leg shot out in a flash, kicking the old dog in the belly so hard the air in the library was shattered by a pitiful yelp. Daisy cowered and slunk under a nearby table. The girls scrambled to the floor, crooning words of love and caressing the quivering creature. Daisy licked their hands, and in no time, her tail began wagging.

Napoleon did not react in any way, and Zelda did not allow her astonishment to show.

# Chapter Five

Recently, the O'Neils had added a covered porch running the whole width of the house. Although it took up most of the backyard, the long railing was a perfect place to mount window boxes, which were now overflowing with fragrant herbs and trailing white geraniums.

The day after the luncheon on Park Avenue, Abigail took Phoebe and Chloe to the beach, leaving Zelda with strict instructions to feel and think while swinging in the hammock on what her mother called the new veranda.

Zelda happily complied with the second part of this order, propelling herself back and forth with one leg slung over the side. She flipped idly through various magazines and managed to avoid the first part of the instruction for half an hour or so before being confronted by a parade of childhood memories. The sweetness of nostalgia swept her back decades in time. She wallowed in blissful reminiscences until recalling leaving Adelphi University after only three years to work for Silverman in Manhattan. She sat up straight, furrowing her brow trying to focus on the details of that time.

Lulu Weld, who'd been her best friend and next-door neighbor since first grade, blossomed while completing a two-year degree at Queensborough Community College. She'd gone from being a shy bespectacled girl to a confident, competent professional administrator. Her goal had been to work on Wall

Street, and she was lucky enough to be a one-interview wonder landing at Silverman two weeks after graduating from QCC. Her thick honey-colored curls bounced when she walked with determination, surveying her new domain.

For a whole year, Lulu regaled Zelda with stories of an exciting office filled with brilliant young men. She said there was a tiny apartment in the East Village they could share, if only Zelda had a good income, like hers, and convinced her working at Silverman had much more potential than working for an airline.

There was a job opening in reception, which Lulu's friend in HR had told her about. It didn't take much convincing for Zelda to have an interview, and much to the anguish of her parents, Zelda took the offered position, moving to Manhattan as soon as her exams ended in late May.

Nick spotted her on day one. He'd graduated from Yale the previous June and was working at Silverman as an analyst before applying to business school.

Lulu was seeing Roger Feldman, who'd graduated at the top of Nick's class. Roger was headed for Harvard Business School in the fall, but he had *not* invited her to move with him to Cambridge. Lulu was crazy about Roger, but felt she would be doing herself a favor to disentangle from him as soon as possible. Her theory had been that there would be three months less for her to fall even further in love.

Zelda recalled that tumultuous summer, remembering the constant on and off with Roger and Lulu and the on and more on with Nick and herself. She smiled as she thought of all the high drama when Roger left for Boston, knowing the outcome from her present perspective.

It was in November that a repentant Roger returned to New York begging Lulu to move in with him. He'd already arranged for a job interview for her at the Widener Library and assured her she would love living in Cambridge. Roger's offer was irresistible to Lulu, and this is how it happened that Nick and Zelda started living together. Economic realities pushed the inevitable along nicely.

While looking back at those early days, Zelda experienced the dizzying lightness of love. It felt brand new again. The feeling was so strong, it was as if she and Nick were connected by an unseen force. She thought if she phoned him now, he would answer immediately, that he was somehow waiting for her call. She pressed his name on her phone and was breathless as the number rang and rang. After the sound of the beep, she said with a catch in her voice, "Hey, You. Just thinking about Astor Place days. Give me a call."

Restlessly, she prowled the porch and then went inside to rummage through a drawer near the kitchen phone. Finding her mother's old address book, she checked under 'W' and pressed the half-remembered numbers. Julia Weld's voice sounded just as it always had, her Louisiana accent having triumphed over time and place.

"Mrs. Weld, it's Zelda. I'm at my parents' for a few days. Just calling to find out what's new with Lulu and Roger."

"Why, Miss Zelda Pie, as I live and breathe. Bring your pretty face over here, and I'll tell all and illustrate it with astounding photos."

"I'll be there in five minutes." Zelda swept her auburn hair into a ponytail, slipped on some sandals and ran to the Weld's.

With a glass of iced tea in hand and a plate of peanut butter cookies in front of her, Zelda nestled into the plump cushions of the same sofa she'd sat on so often as a teenager. The nap of the blue velvet was worn, and Mrs. Weld had a few more lines on her fine-boned face, but her dark brown eyes were as bright as ever, her smile as welcoming.

Zelda launched in, "I'm ashamed to say, I've lost touch with Lulu. Her not having Internet at the kibbutz makes it so hard, and I have four kids, five and under..."

"Darlin', you don't have to tell *me* how hard it is keepin' up with Lulu. For years, I wrote these letters and put these stamps on them and searched for active mailboxes. I felt like I was right back in the Twentieth Century. But they're living in Jerusalem now. It's all very Twenty-first Century there."

"Tell me everything."

"No kids yet, but Lulu has converted to Judaism so she can be a real Jewish mama, just in case, and Roger's in rabbinical school. He had some sort of awakening on the kibbutz and is going to become a real rabbi next spring."

"Get out. Will they come back to the States?"

"Apparently, there's a severe shortage of rabbis in New York. Thank God."

"They've been there a long time. Longer than I've been in California."

"Doug and I went over twice, but they haven't come home at all. Lulu speaks Hebrew now, can you believe it?"

"Lulu can do anything she sets her mind to. You know that, Mrs. Weld. Now show me the photos."

They sat side by side and studied dozens of photographs of Lulu and Roger in Israel and dozens more on Zelda's phone of Nick and the kids. Shadows lengthened and day faded softly into evening, adding a conspiratorial charm to the figures hunched over the screen.

The ring of Zelda's phone made both women jump. Zelda answered and assured her mother she'd be home shortly while Julia Weld turned on some lights.

"Doug won't be able to see that golf ball at all soon. Can you stay and say 'hello'?" Julia scrutinized the sky through the picture window.

"I'd love to, and I want to hear how Father Bobby took Lulu's conversion."

"I haven't got the balls to tell him. Neither does Doug. I told him about Roger going to the seminary, though. He got a big kick out of that. Roger, the adamant atheist."

"It doesn't really surprise me. Lulu wasn't about to let him get away without at least investigating the possibility of God."

"Well, he's got God now, or God's got him. And for whatever good it'll do him, he's got all that money he made at Silverman safe here in the US. He'll be the richest rabbi in the world."

"I wouldn't count on that, if I were you."

Doug Weld's arrival interrupted these musings, and Zelda left with a promise to see them again before she returned to California, but a constant round of family events intervened, and she never made good on that promise.

On the flight back to San Francisco, Zelda tried to imagine telling Nick that his mother seemed in need of some help. It was too difficult. No image of this was forthcoming. There were no clothes in her enormous closets appropriate for making this announcement. She realized that not only was her wardrobe deficient, but her personality was not up to the job, either.

She considered what her moral responsibility was, if any, in alerting Nick to his mother's circumstances, but then she asked herself, what were those circumstances, exactly? Well, Francesca had not been replaced, the paint was peeling and things were dingy. That didn't add up to a hill of beans when she thought about it. It was kicking Daisy that was the real shocker.

It didn't matter that she couldn't imagine herself delivering this report. It was an impossibility. She may look like an O'Neil on the outside, but she didn't have the "I chopped down the cherry tree" type backbone the others had. She squirmed beneath the seat belt. She could never address it. She knew it and felt like an imposter. Any of her siblings would relish the opportunity to sound the opening salvo of what would surely be a life-changing confrontation. But not Zelda.

# Chapter Six

By the time Brooke returned from Wyoming, Zelda had settled into the laziness of August. The foghorns sang their lullabies, the mist billowed into soft blankets around her, and her camellia bushes were budding up nicely, preparing for their fall display. Phoebe and Chloe had play dates and day camp, and even the twins had an occasional birthday party to attend. Nick was considerate and jocular, no criticism, no demands, and if it weren't for an underlying awareness that all this could collapse abruptly, Zelda would say she had everything she'd ever dreamed of.

She started an email correspondence with Lulu in this mood and writing about her present happiness intensified it, heightening her attentiveness to the things that contributed to this sense of ease and contentment. She wrote about the energy of her children, their humor and love. She wrote that loving them had swelled her heart and made room for so much more. Writing this stung her eyes, and she quickly switched to praise for San Francisco, her house and Lourdes. She wrote that Nick was just the same and promised a reunion when the Feldmans got back to New York. She pushed send without re-reading for typos.

Brooke's demanding hostess jitters came jolting through the phone daily. Finally Zelda said, "Dr. Lloyd specifically said to call her after Labor Day with the date. I don't want to hound her."

"But what if she's busy on the second?"

"Then you'll change the date. I'm sure your horoscope holds other propitious days in October."

"But…."

"Stop, Brooke. You're driving us both crazy."

"On top of this, no one invited us to Tahoe for Labor Day weekend."

"We weren't invited either. So what?"

"We should have our own houses there. We're married to such losers."

"Brooke! We're definitely not married to losers. Now tell me what's the matter. Come on, full disclosure."

"Liane said soon there'll be a Saturn pass over my moon, and I absolutely *have* to have this luncheon while the sun is still in Libra."

Sensing she was defeated by Saturn's transit, Zelda said, "I'll call Dr. Lloyd tomorrow. She may not be back from wherever she went. But I'll try."

A young–sounding voice answered the professor's line and convinced Zelda that there was no way to contact Dr. Lloyd until Monday, August twenty-ninth, at which time she could be counted on to be back at Stanford. And no, there wasn't any way to know whether the professor was available for lunch on October second, but there were no classes scheduled that day.

This information mollified Brooke, and she directed her attention elsewhere. Since the Duncans and the Blairs would, alas, be in town, over Labor Day, Brooke wanted to ensure they had a great table at a good restaurant and made reservations at La Folie. By the time they met at the restaurant, Brooke was giddy with relief. The date had been confirmed with Dr. Lloyd. She would come to the Duncan's house with three PhD candidates, and they would stay for lunch.

Arriving at the restaurant on the Saturday of Labor Day Weekend, Zelda noticed Brooke had made every effort to look her best. She wore an emerald green silk dress, which showed off her long shapely legs and her fortieth birthday present from Stuart dangled from her ears. The impressive pair of diamond pendants cast twinkling shafts of light punctuating her lovely face.

As they walked through the front room of the restaurant, Brooke murmured to no one in particular, "Surprisingly empty for a Saturday night. But then, anyone who can afford a house in Tahoe is there."

Stuart didn't miss a beat and replied, "I can afford a house in Tahoe, and I'm here."

"If you really can, then we'd better be in that house by this time next year, *buddy*."

Zelda was taken aback by Brooke's tone. She'd only ever seen Brooke the adoring wife, maybe too adoring, come to think of it.

There was a magnum of Perrier-Jouët Fleur cooling on their table, and Stuart asked, "What are we celebrating?"

"We aren't celebrating. We're compensating." The hard edge was still in Brooke's voice.

This tiny peek at a chink in the Duncan marriage was over in a flash. Zelda watched Brooke marshal her forces and re-present herself as the perfect Silverman wife, flattering and amusing the men, sure of her role, sure of her success.

In both the Blair and Duncan households, the whole month of September was taken up by organizing the school year with extracircular activities as well as much too frequent discussions about the book club meeting, agitated on one side, soothing on the other.

Brooke called at the end of September finding Zelda still in bed and announced, "I've made arrangements with one of the musicians, and he'll take lots of photographs with his phone.

Plus he has a friend at our fave mag. They're going to run a six page spread on us."

"Donna's not going to like it."

"Too bad."

Zelda slipped her phone in the pocket of her robe and headed for the kitchen. She grabbed her laptop and slid onto the sofa. Resting her head on the arm, she balanced the computer on her knees and hit compose.

"Dear Lulu,

"I have a friend here named Brooke (you wouldn't like her), but she's beautiful, smart and full of imagination. Recently she showed me her marriage was not what I thought it was, and today I saw she's bound and determined to get the press to report our book club meeting which will irritate at least half the members, the founder most of all. The weird thing is, I thought Brooke admired this woman and wanted to emulate her. And I thought having the book club women like her was high on her endless list of the Most Important Things in Life.

"Brooke's full of paradoxes – dissatisfied and yearning, yearning for the moon yet complacent and proud at the same time. She was raised like we were, but in Florida. Her husband's really successful, and she has EVERYTHING (and flaunts it) but always wants more - more praise, more friends, more jewels, more houses, more men. Maybe even Nick."

Zelda deleted the email and tossed the computer onto a nearby table.

October second finally came, and the calls from Brooke started at 5 a.m. Zelda was afraid she would find Brooke a hyperventilating mess, but when she arrived, at ten, an hour in advance of the meeting, Brooke was cool and in charge of the complicated logistics of hosting a Regency luncheon. It was like being on a movie set with Brooke as the director.

The costumes, wigs and musical instruments were flawless. The only jarring element was the modern footwear on the otherwise perfectly dressed staff. Amazingly, Brooke didn't mind. "You won't be able to tell in the photographs. That's all that counts," she said.

Brooke was dressed as the soul of discretion in a beige Armani pantsuit, but hugging her wrist was a bracelet with an Imperial Russian pedigree. Centered on an intricately worked gold chain were a large old mine diamond and an equally large natural pearl. Brooke told Zelda that Tsar Nicolas the First had presented it to his brother's wife on their wedding day in 1848. It was chic and understated as well as impressive, even without the history.

The members of the book club started drifting in at ten-thirty. No one was expecting what they found, and the reactions were admiration and wonder, highly satisfactory to Brooke. Once the initial surprise had worn off, the women inspected every detail and were thrilled with the perfection of it all. Knowing the meeting started at eleven, they understood that meant being seated with pen in hand by that time, but the chatter continued. Zelda thought they sounded eager, like birds waking at dawn.

Precisely at eleven, the doorbell rang, and Dr. Grace Lloyd with her rebellious wad of gray-streaked red hair, athlete's body and Coke bottle wire-rims burst through the door flanked by two slender young women clutching stacks of notebooks to their chests. They were trailed by a distinguished-looking man, with cropped salt-and-pepper hair, wearing a blue blazer and dark brown Docksiders. Though his hair had more salt than pepper, he moved like an athlete.

Zelda and Brooke were standing in the entrance hall, which was crowded with musicians and their instruments. "Which one of you is Dr. O'Neil's daughter," Dr. Lloyd asked. She sounded like she had lockjaw.

Zelda came forward with her hand extended. "Zelda Blair, Dr. Lloyd. We're so glad you're here."

Dr. Lloyd looked around and said, "Dearie, I'm floored by all the trouble you've gone to. Are you part of a Janeite sect?"

"Let me introduce our hostess, Brooke Duncan."

Brooke put her arm around Dr. Lloyd's shoulders. Body language made it clear this was not welcome, and Brooke recovered by saying, "We're on a Jane Austin bender this year, and I wanted to set the mood."

"Well, you've certainly succeeded." Grace Lloyd adjusted her glasses then presented the PhD candidates, and they proceeded into the living room.

Once everyone had settled down, Brooke made the appropriate introduction. Then Dr. Lloyd took over.

"Good morning, ladies. I guess we all love time travel, and I'm surprised and delighted to find myself in Regency England with you today. We're going to discuss Miss Austin's emphasis on feminine frivolity and how it provides humor as well as stresses the plight of women of the day. In about an hour, we'll take a few questions on this subject."

During the lively discussion that followed, Dr. Lloyd's zany personality captivated the audience. Her use of antiquated slang was a real crowd pleaser and calling everyone 'dearie' was, well, endearing. Zelda was drawn to Eli Russell, the only man in a house full of women. He was quiet but when he spoke his comments were profound and delivered with wry wit.

During the Q and A, the questions were more about flaunting intellects than curiosity. The women were interested in impressing each other and viewed Dr. Lloyd more as a madcap accessory to the Jane Austen theme than as the highly regarded scholar that she was. The irony of this was not lost on the Stanford consortium.

The caterers had done their research and small stemmed-glasses of Madeira and elderberry wine were passed, and by the time luncheon was announced, everyone was in high spirits.

They started with autumnal vegetable soup, followed by partridge pie, then salad with cheese timbales, topped off with syllabub and gingerbread. All four courses were accompanied by mead, wine made from honey, prepared by the chef from a Regency recipe. It was dry and slightly sparkling. Coffee and sweetmeats, consisting of sugared-almonds, fruit jellies and flower-shaped marzipan, were served in the living room where the lecture chairs had magically disappeared. The music was a big hit, and it was nearly four o'clock before the guests began leaving. Brooke was triumphant. No one, they all agreed, had ever hosted a more amusing luncheon.

Zelda stayed on after everyone else had departed. "I saw the harpsichordist, or whatever he was, taking plenty of pictures. I don't think anyone else noticed, though. Everyone was so blown away by Dr. Lloyd."

"She's stellar. Please thank your mother for recommending her. Dr. Lloyd said she's looking forward to the May meeting."

"So am I."

Brooke slipped off her heels and flung herself on the sofa. "No one will ever forget today, and I think I'll even be forgiven for the publicity. After all, how could I've known one of the musicians had a friend in the press? Not *my* fault." Brooke was high from her unmitigated success.

"Press?"

"Yes, press."

"Oh, well. Good publicity for Stanlee, McCall's and Bloomers. Your guy got close-up shots of the flowers, I noticed, and I bet he was in the kitchen during the meeting."

"He was. It was all part of the deal."

"The deal?" Zelda hoped she didn't sound as unsettled as she felt.

"There's always a deal, Zelda. Don't you know that? Not to change the subject, but I saw you and Eli Russell talking non-stop after lunch. I read about him in *San Francisco Today*. He started faux.com and sold it privately for an undisclosed, but purportedly, enormous number."

"Really? All he talked about were his passions for Jane Austen and the burrowing owl. He says he splits his time between the two. He didn't mention anything else."

"I guess he thought AI conversations would clash with the décor."

"Which, by the way, is sensational. Even though I knew all the plans, it was still exciting. Patrick certainly knows how to set the scene."

"It's good." Brooke nodded her head, surveying the room. "Stuart will be pleased."

# Chapter Seven

The next week *San Francisco Today* dedicated the cover and eight full pages in the center of the magazine to "Austentation in San Francisco." It was noted that the waitstaff was composed of actors who were comfortable in Regency dress and that the musicians were schooled at Julliard.

The article went on to quote an anonymous source claiming blue pansies were grown especially for the party. "Pansies are not a commercial flower yet were a Regency favorite. Brooke Duncan wanted authenticity and was not counting the cost."

Brooke took the magazine to her room and stretched out on her bed to savor every image, every word. After having feasted on it for a full hour, she picked up her cell and called Zelda. "Have you seen the mag? It's perfect. I don't know how Abe got such good photographs on his phone."

"Donna's not going to like it." Zelda had seen the magazine and was worried about what Dr. Lloyd would think of being featured as part of such an extravaganza, but as the magazine pointed out, a luncheon on this scale provided work for many.

"Do you think I should call her and say I have no idea how this got leaked?"

"I wouldn't. The less said to Donna on this subject, the better. But consider what you might say in case she calls you."

"I'll think about it," Brooke replied.

Zelda said, "Don't make the first move."

Brooke ended the call and immediately hit Donna Hall's name on her screen.

"Good morning, Donna. This is Brooke, and I'm very red in the face. I can't think who could have taken all those photographs. None of us would ever want any press coverage for our group."

"Save your breath, Brooke. My family's contacts run deep in this town, and I've known about it from the beginning. I could've stopped you, but as the article said, it was good business for many people. It was beautiful and provided an opportunity to showcase local talent. You're a very generous lady."

Brooke stalled, her face hot now. "You, too, are generous. I'm sorry." She slid her feet to the floor.

"Don't ever use the book club for self-promotion again. But please continue giving your wonderful parties."

Brooke sat still at the edge of her bed. She felt as if she had suffered a direct hit from some unidentifiable heavy object. She recognized it could have been much worse, but the wind had been knocked out of her, and she would need some time to recover.

Calls came in from Stuart and many of the book club members, but she let them go to voicemail. On this day of her great triumph, she had to remain silent and still. It was all too clear to her that it was Donna who had seen *her* and raised her one this time.

Brooke watched the last rays of afternoon sun slide down the wall of her bedroom and pool on the glistening teak floor. She knew it was now time to rally. She'd have to seem exhilarated for Stuart and the girls, so she showered and dressed for a celebration.

She knew Nick and Stuart would have perused the magazine at work and figured they'd want to take their wives out somewhere nice for dinner. It would be a challenge to get a last minute table at Gary Danko's, but not an insurmountable one.

The two couples were asked to wait at the bar in the popular restaurant as their table was being prepared. To the left of Brooke sat Eli Russell. She recognized him right away. "Mr. Russell, so nice to see you again." The heads of the three others turned with interest towards Eli.

"Good evening, Mrs. Duncan. I read all about your wonderful party in *San Francisco Today*." His voice sounded neither judgmental nor enthusiastic.

Stuart Duncan jumped right in. "Call us Stuart and Brooke. My wife told me you are a PhD candidate and a fan of Jane Austen."

Eli nodded but didn't reply.

"Why don't you join our table, if you are alone," Stuart said.

Eli looked at Zelda as he said, "I'd love to join you."

Stuart and Nick vied for Eli's attention all evening, but as they were leaving, Eli managed to whisper to Zelda, "Let's have lunch and talk about owls and literature."

They were about the same height and stood for a second making eye contact. Eli continued, "I'll be in touch." Zelda said nothing and managed to keep her facial expression neutral.

She felt the blood rush to her abdomen. It felt like butterflies, just like they say in romance novels. She couldn't suppress the hint of a smile forming on her lips, an involuntary reaction to his words.

A few days later she got an email from Eli explaining that he had her email address as they were both copied on the confirmation Dr. Lloyd sent concerning Brooke's luncheon. He added that he was out of the country. "I'll be back after Thanksgiving, and I'm looking forward to seeing YOU." Zelda was thrilled and disappointed. Thanksgiving seemed a long way away.

At the end of October, Marion Blair called her daughter-in-law. Zelda was on her way to pick up Phoebe from ballet class when the call came through, and Marion's voice filled her SUV.

"Zelda, dear, it would be so nice of you to have me for Thanksgiving this year. With Francesca back in Portugal, and Napoleon getting on in years, I can't entertain like I used to."

"You're certainly welcome, but my mother will be here. There's a nice hotel nearby."

"I'm a woman alone. Can't your parents go to the hotel?"

"Dad will be in London. He's being honored by Scotland Yard. Mom's been planning to come for over six months. She's staying in our only guest room."

"Well, you don't have to be so disagreeable. And I'm sure you can squeeze me into that big house. Please don't forget who pays."

Zelda took a deep breath. There had been innuendos along these financial lines over the years, but Marion had never been so blatant.

"There's that sewing room off the kitchen we could make up," Zelda said.

"Since your mother's younger, I'm sure she'd be more comfortable there than I would. I'll be arriving on Tuesday in time for dinner and departing on Monday morning. Plane reservations are hard to get at this time of year so there'll be no changes."

Zelda was left with her mouth open. She thought for a moment about whom she could count on to indulge in some moral indignation with her. No one in San Francisco, she admitted to herself. She went home and composed an email to Lulu but deleted it before sending.

What she could do was plan a dinner with Dr. Lloyd. Marion would surely be uncomfortable with two professors discussing literature. Zelda felt better thinking she'd make it her business to keep the conversation intellectually heavy all evening and do her best to make it hell on earth for Marion.

Invigorated by this plan, she went to her bedroom to call the professor.

When Nick came home Zelda reported, "I've invited Dr. Lloyd for supper on Friday after Thanksgiving. My mother will be here, as you know, and your mother is coming as well."

"Yeah, she called me. This would be a perfect time to invite Eli Russell. I think I could do some business with him."

Zelda came close to saying he wouldn't be in town. "He's not...in my contacts. I'll find out how to reach him from Dr. Lloyd."

"Move on this. I want to get to him before Stuart does."

"I only have her office number. I'll call in the morning."

The next afternoon, Nick followed up. "Did you get Eli Russell?"

"He's out of town and not expected back until after Thanksgiving."

"I can't imagine my mother will have much in common with your Dr. Lloyd. Can't we save her for when we get Eli?"

"Try not to forget that we know Dr. Lloyd and, therefore, Eli because my mother is an English professor. She and Dr. Lloyd have a *great* deal in common. It will be an interesting evening. I'm sure your mother will find it fascinating."

"Forget it. She'll hate it. But do your best to give Dr. Lloyd a good time. You'll need her as an excuse to get Eli Russell over as soon as he gets back."

That night she got a swift kick on the flank followed by tender lovemaking. In the morning there was swelling, which she decided to ignore.

Later in the day an email from Eli arrived. "Back Thanksgiving night. Want to see you soon and often."

Zelda replied: "Dr. L. coming for dinner here on Friday. Why don't you come, too?"

"Sold. What time?"

"Seven."

Zelda left a message on Nick's cell that Eli would be able to come for dinner on Friday after Thanksgiving after all. Almost right away, Zelda saw an incoming call from Nick but let it go to voicemail. Later she listened to the message twice.

"There's been a screw-up. Stuart and I have to leave for Hong Kong on Thanksgiving night. Turn your charm on Russell. He *has* to want to come back. Plan another dinner with him before Christmas. Be sure he comes." There was a threatening quality to the message, which was not lost on Zelda.

# Chapter Eight

As it turned out, Marion Blair and Abigail O'Neil arrived in San Francisco on the same plane. Zelda was waiting in baggage claim with Phoebe and Chloe, and by the time they arrived home, Nick was there to open the door with a twin in each arm.

Nick laid on the charm for the two older women and seemed genuinely happy to be their host at home on Tuesday night and at his club on Wednesday. Zelda had hired a chef to prepare the traditional fare on Thanksgiving and have it ready to serve at 2 p.m. Another family with similarly aged children joined them, and even though Marion Blair had several martinis, all went well until coffee was being served in the living room.

Leaning over his mother, who was slightly slumped in a wing chair, Nick whispered, "Mom, would you like me to help you to your room?"

Marion rallied and made every effort to slug her son in the face and kick him in the shins, but she didn't have the strength to do any damage. Thinking no one had witnessed this, Nick apologized to her, took her arm and guided her upstairs.

Zelda's throat tightened with compassion for Nick. What a childhood he must have had, she thought, and hugged Chloe to her chest.

As it turned out, Marion did not come down to see Nick off that evening and stayed in her room until the following morning.

The next day, Zelda was determined not to let Marion ruin her mood, and when her mother-in-law appeared in the kitchen, she said cheerfully, "Good morning, Marion, I hope you slept well."

"Very well, thanks. I take it Nick got off all right. I'm looking forward to that butterfly exhibit and tea at Lovejoy's with the girls today."

"I won't be joining you, but Lourdes will take you in the Tesla, and I'll run my errands in Nick's car. Professor Grace Lloyd, Eli Russell and the Miller's from across the street are expected at seven. You'll like them."

"You'll be glad to know I read all of Miss Austen's novels when I was in school, so I won't embarrass you in front of your professor friend. And Nick told me he'd like to do business with Eli Russell. I'm expected to work my magic on him."

"You always can be counted on for that, can't you?" Zelda raised an eyebrow.

"I feel I'm representing Nick tonight."

"Okay then. We'll do our best to entertain Eli. Now, what can I fix you for breakfast?"

"Never anything but black coffee for me."

When Abigail arrived on the kitchen scene, she barely acknowledged Marion, which left Zelda wondering if her mother had witnessed the incident with Nick and Marion the night before.

Abigail turned to her daughter and asked, "What can I do to help you with dinner tonight?"

"Everything's under control, Mom. Why don't you and Marion take the twins for a walk? There's plenty of time before lunch, and after that you two can take the girls for their outing."

Accepting the situation with as much grace as she could muster, Abigail said, "We'll get out of your hair, and let you get on with it. Come on, Marion. Finish your coffee. Matt and Miles need to get to know their grannies."

Unwilling to be rushed, Marion asked for a second cup before they took the twins out. Zelda flew through her day, excited and apprehensive about seeing Eli.

Eli Russell lived in Atherton, where a cluster of palaces house the Sultans of Silicon Valley. The drive to Pierce Street would be about an hour, and he called Grace to offer her a ride to Zelda's dinner. It would be twenty minutes out of his way, but he enjoyed her company.

The two literature professors found each other hilarious and kept the table in peals of laughter. Even Marion was enjoying herself, and the lurking tension between Zelda and Eli dissolved before dessert.

Zelda had prepared a chocolate soufflé. Fallen and over-cooked, this culinary disaster was the cause of more laughter, and everyone sat around the table chatting and putting soufflé sauce into the coffee. Delicious. The sauce was heated vanilla ice cream, a perfect addition to the bitter brew.

Four-year-old Phoebe wandered in, barefoot, wearing pajamas and whispered something in Zelda's ear. Marion's eyes narrowed and the muscles in her arm tensed as if she were about to raise it in a menacing way. It was over in an instant, but Zelda sensed Abigail and Grace had seen it. She thought she'd caught a glance between them.

Eli and Grace were the first to leave as they had the farthest to go. Though not a lot was said between Eli and Zelda, their attraction to each other hadn't been lost on Grace. Seated in the passenger seat of Eli's Jeep Grand Cherokee, Grace opened the window and said to the great outdoors, "I wonder why Eli never said a word to Zelda."

"I was only invited because of you. I don't know Zelda at all," Eli muttered.

Clucking in disbelief, Grace said, "You sat across from the mother-in-law. What did you think of her?"

"A harmless old bat. Self-satisfied and uninteresting."

"Did you see her consider walloping her granddaughter?"

"What?"

"You were too busy watching the mother-child vignette to notice anything."

"Explain yourself, Grace."

"I think there's a violent streak in Marion. Not a harmless old bat after all, but a venomous old spider."

Eli took his eyes off the road and for a moment stared at Grace. "Tell me more."

"There's nothing more to tell at present. But I think there's something gravely wrong with her. I'm glad Abigail is there."

"You don't think Marion would hurt anyone, do you?"

"All I can tell you is that hatred filled her face and her right arm for a moment when the child was whispering to Zelda."

"Do you think we should go back there?"

"And do what, dearie? Offer our protection?"

"I think you should warn Abigail."

"She saw," Grace said quietly while staring at the moon. They remained silent for the rest of the drive to Woodside.

Driving up to Grace's house, Eli cleared his throat, "Grace, I think...."

"Relax, dearie. There is nothing you can do. Maybe I'll see Abigail before she goes back to New York. If I do, I'll bring it up."

Eli got out of the car and walked Grace to the door. He leaned down and kissed the top of her head. "Don't forget to warn her. See you Monday."

The next morning brought the whole Blair household plus Brooke with Taylor and Audrey in tow to the family kitchen.

Saturday meant pancakes, and even while griping about Thanksgiving being so fattening, they dipped into second helpings.

After breakfast, Abigail said to Zelda, "I'm going to give Grace a call and see if she's free. I'd love to see the Stanford campus."

"She doesn't live in faculty housing. I think she's in Woodside."

"Is that far?"

"Not for California."

Abigail arrived at Grace's by Uber and said, "What a lovely house! I'm sure you'd rather stay here. The last thing you want to do on Thanksgiving weekend is to lead the Stanford tour."

"Listen, dearie, I don't have many colleagues visiting from Long Island, and I've never found anything I'd rather do than discuss literature with my peers. We're lucky it's not raining. Let's go before the weather changes its mind."

After the tour, they drove back to Grace's house. "Abigail, I hope you won't think I'm meddling, but I think we both saw something troubling last night."

"Marion?" Abigail raised her eyebrows.

"Is Zelda aware?"

"I don't know. But I'm going to find out before I leave."

"Maybe Marion shouldn't be left alone with the children."

"I don't think she has much interest in them, so I doubt there's any chance of that."

"Just so Zelda knows."

Abigail looked at her watch. "Right. Speaking of Zelda, I'd better be getting back."

"Eli lives near here. Let me call him. He can drive you back."

"Don't bother him."

"If he's not out spying on the burrowing owl, I'm sure he'd welcome a break from the computer," Grace said while pressing Eli's name on her phone.

"Eli, get over here and drive Abigail back to Zelda, please." Grace turned back to Abigail. "He's on his way."

It occurred to Abigail that Eli must have known of this assignment in advance, but no mention was made.

Calling Zelda from the car, Abigail said Eli was driving her and they'd be arriving around 6:30.

"If Eli can bear it, he'd be welcome to stay for supper."

Eli allowed as how he could bear it and accelerated up the 280 towards San Francisco.

Abigail noticed that Zelda was unusually animated that evening and was relieved Marion seemed completely unaware of anyone other than herself and Eli. Also Abigail thought it odd that both Marion and Zelda appeared to be flirting with Eli. And all the while, Eli was concentrating on making dragon puppets for the children out of the green napkins, oblivious of both women. He made a quiet exit while Zelda was putting the children to bed.

Eli texted later that night. "Two nice dinners. Thanks so much."

Holding her phone out for her mother to see, Zelda said, "He doesn't seem very enthusiastic."

"Do you want him to be?"

"Of course not. Just saying." Zelda's voice sounded wooden to Abigail's ears.

The rest of the weekend passed quietly, but the right moment to talk to her mother about Nick's violence never came, nor did the moment for Abigail to talk to Zelda about Marion present itself. Unspoken words whispered and shouted in an unending round through the minds of both mother and daughter.

# Chapter Nine

Marion and Abigail returned to New York on Monday, and on Thursday Nick came home from Hong Kong. He dropped his bags off at the house on his way to the office and found Zelda in their bedroom. The first thing he wanted to know was if she'd made arrangements for Eli to come for dinner again.

"No, I haven't. I don't want him to think we're pursuing him," she said tersely.

"We *are* pursuing him, Zelda. I want him as a client, don't you get it?"

"You call him, then."

He gave her a half-hearted kick and left for work.

"I'm so sorry, Nick," Zelda said softly to his retreating back.

"You ought to be," was Nick's retort. He didn't bother to turn around.

Zelda busied herself with the children for the rest of the day, and barely remembered the kick by the time Nick came home. He was in a good mood as the trip to Hong Kong had resulted in big business for the firm. He and Stuart were the stars of the moment.

As if nothing had happened, Nick said, "We're going out with the Duncans to celebrate."

"I would've thought you and Stuart would be jet lagged."

"Never. Get ready. We're going to Battery."

The two couples arrived at the club at the same time and were shown to their table where the women sat on the banquette facing the main dining room. Stuart ordered a bottle of Cristal and just as the waiter presented it, Zelda spotted Eli with a beautiful blonde a few tables away.

Seeing him at the same moment, Brooke touched Stuart's hand. "There's Eli Russell with Donna Hall's older sister."

Zelda's heart sank, but Nick's enthusiasm was irrepressible. "Maybe they'd like to join us."

Stuart signaled to the waiter to pour the Champagne and said, "Forget it.

He's not interested in us tonight."

Zelda couldn't concentrate on the conversation at her table. Try as she might to stay focused, her eyes kept straying to Eli, whose attention never wavered from his date. Zelda ordered Crêpes Suzette for dessert thinking the burst of flames would draw his eyes to her, but by the time the match was struck, Eli's table was empty. She caught a glimpse of his perfectly straight back as he disappeared from the room.

The next morning Brooke called Zelda. "They met on the internet."

Pretending unawareness, Zelda demurred, "Who met on the internet?"

"Eli and Elaina Hall."

"*How* do you find these things out?"

"I have my sources."

"They looked like they were enjoying each other's company last night," Zelda ventured.

"It was their first date. They're certainly well suited. This could be big."

Zelda did her best to sound cheerful and ended by agreeing to meet Brooke for lunch at Cultivar, even though the last thing she wanted to do was listen to Brooke summarize the news of the day, especially if it included speculating on an Eli-Elaina romance.

Zelda dragged herself through the morning, then at noon set out to meet Brooke. Fastening her seatbelt, she heard her phone ping. The mood-altering text was from Eli: You looked lovely last night.

Nothing that Brooke predicted over lunch could dampen her high.

Nick was later than usual coming home from work. "I talked to Stuart, and he agrees. The sooner we get to Eli Russell, the better. I want him here for dinner before Christmas. The Duncans, us and Eli with Elaina Hall or Professor What's-her-name."

"The Duncans? I thought you wanted Eli for yourself."

"We'll partner in this."

"I've never met Elaina Hall."

"I don't care who he's with, just get him here. And ask that guy who did Thanksgiving to cook."

"Okay. Is there a menu you have in mind?"

Nick missed the sarcasm in her voice, and said, "Yeah, there is. For festive dinners my mother used to have lobster bisque and crown roast of lamb with a hot fruit soufflé for dessert. I want that. I can get some nice wines."

"I'll call Grace now and see what date suits her."

"Eli Russell is the person of interest here, Zelda."

Zelda kept eye contact with Nick as she called Eli. He answered on the first ring. "Eli, Nick and I want you and Grace to come for dinner before the holidays overwhelm us. Are you free sometime next week?"

Moments later, sounding disappointed, Zelda said, "Oh, I see. We'll count on you and Grace after the sixth of January, then. Let's say the tenth."

Turning to Nick, she announced, "He and Grace are going on a three-week cruise to Antarctica. They leave for Argentina tomorrow."

Time flew, and before Zelda knew it, Santa Claus had come and gone. The tree was down, and she was puzzling over the subtle art of table décor. Having decided on glacial white for cloth, napkins and flowers, she searched the Internet for penguin place cards.

Zelda and Brooke knew what to expect from the evening ahead, but Grace, who was the last to arrive, was surprised to find the men had already deserted the women. They were watching a video presentation in the library and continued a business discussion throughout most of dinner. Then the men stayed rooted at the dining table, and the women had coffee in the living room.

Grace held her cup up for more coffee. "Zelda, I'm getting a ride home from Eli. Do you think that'll be any time soon?"

"I'm so sorry. If you're ready, I'll go get him now."

"No. Let them talk. I'm not used to being with members of the financial community. It's good for me to remember that not everyone likes to discuss Nineteenth Century English literature night and day."

"Sometimes Nick and Stuart bore us to death," Brooke chimed in. "But usually they're the life of the party. Right, Zelda?"

"Right, and as for me, I'm always happy if they don't break out the cigars."

"I think we'll be spared that tonight since Eli is allergic," Grace yawned.

"Let's play Scrabble while we wait." Brooke suggested. Both young women were anxious for their husbands to complete their business uninterrupted.

Perking right up, Grace said, "Groovy. Let's play for money."

Zelda looked over at Brooke. They silently agreed. "We've never played for money before, so you'll have to score," Brooke said.

"The faculty lounge has a game going at all times. Watch out. I'm good."

The game went on until nearly midnight. An unheard of hour for San Francisco considering how early the financial community has to arise in order to be in sync with New York.

As for the Scrabble game, Grace was the big winner, ending up with eleven dollars and fifty cents. "You girls are worthy opponents. I'll give you a chance to win your money back anytime."

Eli thanked the Blairs and said, "Great dessert. Never had strawberry soufflé before. Sure beats the chocolate ones I've had lately." There was a conspiratorial grin on his face.

"It was Nick's mother's idea," Zelda offered. The surprise in Eli's eyes made her smile.

After Grace and Eli had departed, despite the late hour, Nick said to Stuart, "Stay for a cigar. Zelda and Brooke can play more Scrabble."

Two days later at noon, Zelda drove past Brooke's house on her way to Pilates and noticed Nick's car was parked a block away. She pressed his cell number. It went directly to voicemail. She called the office and was told he was out for the rest of the day.

Shock was beginning to set in, but she managed to say, "Is Mr. Duncan available, then?"

"I'm sorry, Mrs. Blair. Mr. Duncan is in LA and won't be back in the office until Friday."

Instead of going to her class, Zelda sped home. Running upstairs, burning mad, she called Brooke's landline and cell to no avail. Hot tears sprang from her eyes as she threw herself face down on her bed.

An hour later, having pulled herself together, she tried to think. All she could remember was her senior year when Mrs. Weld said in her honey-dipped accent of the deep South, "Lulu, you and Zelda better choose your men with care. Once you have children, you can't ever get divorced. And not just because you're Catholic. The biological father will always be the best for the kids."

Lulu had stretched and said, "Once the kids are grown, we'd have a second chance."

"Nooo," Mrs. Weld said. "By that time, you'll have way, way too much skin in the game. Mark my words."

Zelda knew her mother held similar views. And she couldn't risk her father finding out. At least not now. With her heart breaking, she realized she had no confidante in California other than Brooke. At this point, she thought she could hear her sense of stability sneaking away.

She went and found the twins who were in the kitchen in their highchairs eating applesauce. She brought them to her room and played peek-a-boo through her silent tears.

# Chapter Ten

O f Zelda's siblings, Hank was the only one unmarried, and at thirty-six, he was the closest to her in age. As usual, she turned to him.

Seeking privacy, Zelda sat alone in her car outside her garage door and called Hank at his office. After recounting the facts, she said, "You know, those times Nick tried his kickboxing moves on me, he never really meant to hurt me." Her voice sounded hollow, not as convincing as she would've liked.

"I heard what you said, and I understand you can't tell Mom and ask her to keep secrets from Dad. And you're right, if he found out, there would be security guards all around you whether you think the kicks were meant to hurt or not."

"I know," Zelda sighed. "And the irony is that the luxury of having Lourdes has resulted in my not really knowing any of the other sandbox moms. But with four kids—five and under, don't forget—I need her if I'm going to be a Silverman executive wife."

"What does that even *mean*, Zelda? Mom had eight of us with no nanny in sight."

"You've seen this house, Hank. It doesn't run itself, you know. And I'm expected to entertain here on a level that just doesn't happen in Bayside. Staying in shape and dressing like a model is part of my job. Not complaining, mind you. Just explaining."

"I wish I had some answers for you. It's hard to believe this Brooke woman is your only friend out there. You had so many friends growing up. What about Lulu? Why don't you call her?"

"I've haven't heard her voice in nearly a decade. I can't just call her up in Jerusalem and lay this on her. And don't forget, Nick and Roger Feldman are friends. Plus the time change makes it hard."

"What about a shrink?"

"I don't have a separate bank account. I seriously doubt Nick would finance me to discuss him with a professional."

"Right. What about Mom's friend? The Jane Austen woman?"

Zelda sighed again, heavily this time. "I don't really know her well enough."

"What if it gets worse? You should definitely pack a suitcase and leave it in your car with the essentials for you and the kids. Social Security numbers, passports, banking information, safety deposit keys and things like that."

"I don't have a lot of 'things like that'. No safety deposit box. The kids don't have passports and mine has probably expired."

"At least you can get valid passports for everyone and plan where to go. Also put aside as much cash as you can and hide it somewhere you can get at it."

"Okay. I'm on it."

"You and the kids are always welcome here, but you know how cramped that'd be."

"Not to mention the three thousand mile drive."

"No, don't bother mentioning that. You need a friend in your time zone."

At that moment her phone signaled an incoming call from Grace Lloyd. "I've got to go. The Jane Austen woman is calling."

"Here's your chance, Zelda. Be nice, now."

She laughed as she accepted the call from Grace.

"Listen, dearie, I'd like to invite you and your husband for dinner. It's Eli's birthday on February first, and though I'm not much of a cook, I do make delicious Beef Stroganoff. You're probably too young to even know what that is. So come and be surprised. And surprise Eli, too."

"Grace, what a great invitation. We'd love to come."

"I'd include the Duncans, but Eli's mother's going to be here, and she's even older than I am. She can't cope with too many people. I'll ask another professor, so we'll be six."

"Where does Eli's mother live?"

"Old Lyme, Connecticut. She's a widow, and Eli's her only child so she comes out here often. She went to Antarctica with us."

"I'll look forward to meeting her. What time do you want us?"

"Seven."

"May I bring the cake?"

"Good idea. I'm a terrible baker."

"Why don't I come early in the afternoon and make the cake in your kitchen?"

"Do that, dearie. I'll get ice cream. I'm good at that."

Zelda called Hank right back. "I'm *in* with the professor. Going for the afternoon and dinner at her place, and if I'm lucky, Nick will be out-of-town."

"Glad to hear it, but I have to get back to work. The DA's office doesn't run itself, you know. Call you tonight."

Later, when Hank called Zelda back, she was in her car again on her way home. "I'm going to make that friend in this time zone. Nick's going to be in Hong Kong, and I'll have Grace Lloyd mostly to myself for twenty-four hours."

"How's that work?"

"She lives in Woodside, which isn't next door. I've offered to bake a birthday cake for a friend of hers at her house. I'll arrive in the early afternoon. Since Nick's away, she invited me to stay the night and go with her to Stanford for lunch the next day."

"What kind of woman is she?"

"Bizarre and brilliant in the best way possible. And very down to earth."

"How old?"

"About Mom's age, I guess."

"Well, good luck with making a friend in a day. Often takes me a bit longer."

"This is an emergency."

"Yeah, it is."

"I'm going to make it happen," Zelda said with conviction.

"I don't doubt it, and I'd be there if I could."

"I love knowing that."

On the morning of the birthday dinner, Zelda shopped for the cake ingredients and packed an overnight case. After lunch with her children, she set off for Grace's. Reaching the address, she found a surprisingly long driveway, which lead to a large A-frame with two small wings on either side. It was painted pale blue with white trim. Zelda picked up the grocery bag and was opening the back of the car when Grace came out.

"Dearie, two suitcases for one night?"

Zelda reddened. "Don't worry. Only the little one comes in with me." She lifted out the small case. "I love your house. Have you lived here long?"

"Twenty-eight years. My blue heaven."

The main room was enormous with four separate areas— sitting room, dining room, library and media. Everything was blue and white. Harmonious, if unimaginative. The kitchen was in the wing with the guest suite, and the two women chatted easily as Zelda unpacked the ingredients.

"How old is the birthday boy?"

"Forty-four," said Grace as she opened the box of candles.

"Did you know him before he became your student?"

"I did, and I like to think he decided to get serious about English Lit thanks to me. I've known him since he was twelve."

"Twelve!"

"I met him in Florida. His parents had taken him to Hobe Sound for spring vacation, and I was there with my family staying at the same inn. He and I took a nature walk. He found a burrowing owl roosting near the golf course."

"Do they really burrow?"

"Sort of. They nest in burrows made by others, like prairie dogs and squirrels, using their beaks to make the nests more comfortable. They have longish legs and walk around quite a lot in the day time, so it's fairly easy to spot them."

"I was wondering why he had such a fascination with them."

"Very rewarding hobby. He's become quite an accomplished photographer and has had articles in all the major nature magazines. I feel like I can claim responsibility for that as well. No end to my hubris, you see."

"What about his mother?"

"She's an elegant lady in her late seventies. She looked like Audrey Hepburn in her youth, and now she looks like you'd imagine Audrey would if she were still with us. Not only that, she's a renowned research endocrinologist. It was her idea that we go to Antarctica. Quite a force to be reckoned with."

"I feel lucky to be included tonight."

Grace patted her hand. "You're doing an important job with your children. I admire you." Sighing, Grace continued, "I regret never having had a family of my own. My one and only true love was killed in Vietnam."

"I'm so sorry."

"Now my students are my children, Eli especially. Without him my life would be the model of banality. A spinster professor, specializing in spinster literature."

"You're the bomb, Grace, and he's the one who's lucky to have you."

"He brings a lot of joy to my life."

"Has he ever been married?" Zelda squinted as she measured out the flour.

"Eli's a lot like me. He had a significant other once. She was killed in a fire, working as a first responder. An explosion… many years ago, now. Her name was Cecelia. A lovely girl."

"Tragic." Zelda stirred in the milk.

"Let's talk about something more cheerful on this propitious day. Tell me about your little ones."

Zelda recounted the various activities of her brood as she made the chocolate cake. While it cooled, she whipped egg whites for the icing, Grace stunned her with the next question.

"And Nick? Do you have anything in common with him other than your children?"

Zelda hesitated.

"I thought not, dearie."

"How could you know? You only met him once."

"It was enough. When someone shows me who they are, I always believe them."

"What do you mean?"

"The other evening's objective was to get Eli in his clutches. It was clear. He's much more Wickham than Darcy."

Going with the *Pride and Prejudice* reference, Zelda laughed, "I hope you're not inferring I'm like Lydia."

"Of course not. You're certainly an Elizabeth, and you deserve a Darcy, not a Wickham."

"You think Nick's as bad as that?"

"Sadly, yes."

For a few moments Zelda said nothing as she dripped sugar syrup slowly into the stiff egg whites. Taking a deep breath, she turned the mixer off and said, "And, sadly, there are a few cracks in our marriage."

"I'm sorry to hear that. But at least your mother's just a phone call away."

"It's hard with the time change. By the time I get the kids to bed, it's late on the east coast."

"Very inconvenient, time changes." Grace paused for a moment. "If you ever need someone to talk to, please feel free to think of me as your west coast confidante."

"I really need a west coast confidante." Zelda threw caution to the winds. "That other suitcase you saw in the car is there in case the children and I need to leave." Zelda surprised herself with the suddenness of the revelation.

Grace paused letting this sink in and then reached over to squeeze Zelda's shoulder affectionately. "Please consider this house a safe place. You're welcome to leave the suitcase here, if you'd like."

Zelda held back her tears and nodded her thanks and acceptance. She was unable to speak for a few moments and then said, "You have no idea how much this means to me."

"I think I do, dearie. We can make a plan in the morning. But now you need to freshen up. Our guests will be here soon."

# Chapter Eleven

Ann Russell took Zelda's breath away. She was slim and petite with silver hair swept back in a simple bun pinned at the nape of her neck. She wore a cream-colored cashmere turtleneck tunic with narrow-legged satin trousers of the same color. Her back was straight, like a dancer's. Zelda had noticed Eli held himself in this way, too.

Ann glided into Grace's house on a cloud of fragrance, something mysterious, which must have been concocted by a master perfumer in the South of France. She smelled like the flower fields in the hills above the Mediterranean Sea. Fresh, strong, invincible.

Her chiseled features were softened by a wide smile, which took over her face on catching sight of Grace. "How is my precious old friend?"

"Dearie, you look younger every time I see you." Grace was not one for hugging and kissing, but she made an exception for Ann.

Eli followed his mother, beaming with evident pride. "Mom played nine holes with me today. Her youthful glow comes from gloating over her win. You're on for tomorrow, Grace. I can't take the humiliation two days in a row."

Still holding Ann's arm, Grace said, "Don't worry, Eli, I'll wipe that smug look off her face, but it can't be tomorrow. I'm having lunch with Zelda and then a seminar in the afternoon."

Zelda was just saying hello to Ann when the two other guests arrived. Rupert and Kirk, professors of Math and Physics, respectively. Rupert was a tall, thin man with a long face and shaggy gray hair. Kirk was tall as well, though stout and bald, with a meticulously groomed graying goatee.

"Dinner will be ready in a flash. Afterwards, I think you math and science people ought to team up and take on us literature people for a punishing game of Scrabble." Grace gestured to the dining table, "Ann, you sit between Rupert and Kirk and get your strategy honed for the game. Zelda, come help me with the salad." Zelda followed Grace into the kitchen.

"Count on Grace to skip cocktails and rush dinner, so she can hustle us into a Scrabble game. We have to let her win. She gets cranky if she loses a cent," Rupert declared.

"Come on, Ru, you know we don't let her win. She's just better, that's all," Kirk said.

"She can't even do entry level Sudoku."

"Now who's cranky?"

Zelda found herself seated next to Eli and not five minutes into the meal she felt his hand searching for hers under the blue tablecloth.

Concentrating on not allowing her face to reflect her confusion, she missed a question directed at her. The next thing she knew, Grace was saying, "Earth to Zelda. Come in, please."

"I'm so sorry. I had an ear infection recently, and I still feel pressure, which makes it hard to hear. Did I miss something?"

"Not much. Kirk wants to know where you're from." Grace piled salad on Eli's plate.

Under the table, Zelda swatted Eli's roving hand while answering the question. "Long Island, born and raised. How about you, Kirk?"

They got through the small talk and the Stroganoff. Before the cake, Grace announced, "I've got Cherry Garcia, Rocky

Road, Peppermint Stick and, best of all, Neapolitan slices. What'll it be, kids?"

Everyone chose ice cream slices, and Zelda presented the cake to Eli with a flourish. Phones came out, recording physical images, but missing the potent chemistry.

The Grace-Eli-Zelda team won at Scrabble, but not by much, only twenty-five cents each. Many words were hotly contested and the Oxford English Dictionary, affectionately known as the OED to the assembled players, was consulted more than usual.

Zelda stood by Grace as the guests were leaving. Eli kissed Grace on the cheek and Zelda on the hand. "Thanks for baking me a cake. My wish is for the same cake made by the same baker every year."

Hiding her pleasure, Zelda said in an off-hand way, "Only if you're lucky."

"I make my luck." Eli took his mother's elbow, walked her outside and helped her into his Jeep.

It was late by the time the kitchen was put to rights, and Grace said, "Get a good night's sleep. Tomorrow you'll make just the right escape plan." Surprising Zelda by giving her a fierce hug, Grace turned off the outside lights and headed to her wing of the house.

The guestroom was upholstered and curtained in French cotton, a light blue background with climbing white roses. The rug was soft and immaculately white. Zelda pulled off her shoes, letting her toes dig deeply into the plush pile.

Zelda slept fitfully and early the next morning tiptoed into the kitchen, not wanting to wake Grace. But there she was, helping herself to a bowl of Cherry Garcia ice cream.

"What a great idea! I'll have the same." Zelda approved of ice cream for breakfast, though she rarely indulged in it.

"Nutritionally, I think it's similar to corn flakes with chocolate milk and a few cherries, don't you?" Grace looked like an owl with her wire-rims, making this sound like esoteric wisdom.

"Definitely, but more festive."

"I usually have ice-cream for breakfast only in summer, but my freezer is full of the stuff. Can't have it going stale."

"Nothing worse than stale Cherry Garcia. I'll finish the pint."

"I have another in case we need more while making your plan."

"Knowing I can leave the suitcase here is a great relief. I was worried Nick would see it. Not that he ever looks in my car, but still…"

Grace handed over an envelope. "Here are the keys to the house and the alarm code, on the off chance the alarm is set. Wifi information is in there, too."

"Grace, are you sure you want to get involved?"

"Don't worry about me. I'm just sorry *you're* involved with whatever this is. If you want to discuss it, you can count on my silence."

"Thanks," Zelda whispered. 'I didn't have anyone here to confide in."

"What about Brooke?"

"I suspect she's having an affair with Nick."

"Oh, dearie. Very awkward."

"Indeed, and Nick sometimes gets a little too rough with me, which I need to keep from my mother. Not fair to tell her, and then ask her not to tell Dad. Dad would overreact, for sure."

Grace shot up and opened the freezer. "We're going to need this," she said while prying off the top and ripping the seal off the back-up Cherry Garcia.

They'd polished off the pint by the time Zelda had finished her tale. She downplayed the attacks and repeated over and over again that Nick could've been in Brooke's neighborhood on firm business, but Grace got the picture.

"Are you afraid Nick will get violent with the children?"

"I don't think he would. And I could be overreacting about this whole thing. Maybe it's really my fault. He's not all that bad. And I could be wrong about Brooke."

"One day, it'll finally be too much, and you'll all come here. There's enough room to bring the nanny, too, if you'd like. One of you can sleep in my home office. There's a pullout. If that day comes, you'll have to tell your parents."

"My brother, Hank, says I should be prepared with passports."

"Hank? Would that be Henry David Thoreau O'Neil?"

"Henry James."

"Ah, one of my faves. I don't think you'll have to flee the country. Although it's a good idea to be prepared for anything."

"I've already started the process."

"Good girl. Now go get that enormous suitcase of yours out of the car and put it under the bed you slept in. We'll take both cars to Stanford because I'm there for the rest of the day."

Arriving home at three o'clock, Zelda found a note from Lourdes on the kitchen table. "Mr. Blair dropped his suitcase off early this morning. He said he'd be home in time for the kids' supper. He says he has a surprise."

Zelda felt guilty that she'd made everyone's favorite cake, and no one at home had gotten a single bite. She had all the ingredients and no excuse. She baked another, and by the time the kids got home, it was out of sight, on top of the refrigerator.

At six-thirty, they sat down and said grace. Zelda was dishing out meatloaf when Nick came in, bearing two large bags filled with wrapped presents.

"We need a little Christmas right this very minute," he sang and placed the bags at the side of his chair. "But first, dinner."

The kids were very excited, but managed to eat enough to satisfy the adults. "Okay, Nick, you go first. Then I have a surprise," Zelda said.

Colorful presents for everyone including Zelda and Lourdes came pouring out of the bags. Scarves for the women, toys and funny masks for the children. Zelda modeled her scarf for everyone, then danced out of the dining room and returned with the cake.

Even though there were no candles on it and no birthday boy or girl, the kids started singing Happy Birthday, ending with, "Happy Birthday, dear Daddy," as Zelda placed the cake in front of Nick.

The whole cake disappeared before they trudged upstairs for nighttime rituals.

Later, from the kitchen, Zelda texted Grace. "I feel so disloyal. Nick can be so much fun and is such a good father. Please forget what I told you. Also forgive me for consuming all your time, sympathy and Cherry Garcia."

She padded upstairs, had a bath and smoothed on her sumptuous crème brulée-scented body cream. After brushing her hair, she slipped into her skimpiest nightie and slid cautiously under freshly laundered linen sheets, waiting.

# Chapter Twelve

While sitting at the breakfast table the next morning, Zelda heard her phone ping. She reached for it and read, "Where there's smoke, there's fire, dearie."

Nick read the message, too, as he leaned down to kiss Zelda on top of her head. He remarked, "Is that from the professor? What does she mean by that?"

Zelda clenched and thought quickly. "Who knows? Something about a Scrabble game, I think."

"Right. I remember you girls had a hot game a couple of weeks ago." Fortunately, he lost interest in Zelda's message from Grace and concentrated on Chloe's rendition of "Row, Row, Row Your Boat."

Zelda silenced her phone and slipped it into the pocket of her robe, not to be touched until Nick had left the house. Zelda re-read the message, and she wondered if Nick's guilty feelings about Brooke could be the reason for the unexpected presents. Then, "I'm just paranoid," flickered through her brain.

Those two thoughts ricocheted back and forth all day. Finally, she texted Grace back. "Are you free to talk?"

"Will call in a few minutes."

Their conversation ended with Grace saying, "I'd like to invite myself over for dinner some night this week when Nick's home. Let's not complicate things by inviting Eli and Ann unless you think it's absolutely necessary."

"Okay. I think he's here all week. How about tomorrow?"

"I can be there by seven."

Zelda was almost asleep by the time Nick got home that night. Although groggy, she remembered Grace. "I asked the professor for dinner tomorrow night. Can you be home in time?"

"Yes, but I don't want to have to have dinner with her alone. It's a good excuse to have Eli."

"His mother's in town."

"Invite her, too. And the Duncans. Text me how many can make it. I'll get the wine. Eli said his favorite is Swanson's Alexis Cabernet Sauvignon. Plan your main dish around that. What about your roast duck?"

Zelda mumbled her assent. This will be interesting, she thought, as she dozed off.

Eli and Ann were happy to accept the Blair's invitation. And so were the Duncans.

Zelda called Grace. "It was absolutely necessary to ask Eli and Ann. Plus the Duncans. I can't wait for your take on the Nick-Brooke situation. Maybe I'm way off base."

"I'll analyze the state of affairs. Don't worry. I'm really good at this. I could've been a spy."

"I'm sure you could've been a lot of things, Grace."

"I'm tenured now so I'm sticking with this gig. Speaking of which, I think you should finish your college degree and consider a career after you've raised your kiddies."

"I know I should. But I'm too busy."

"We'll think of a way."

That night, Grace arrived before Nick got home to help Zelda with the finishing touches to the meal. Zelda had prepared a bitter orange sauce for the duck along with sweet potatoes and roasted Brussels sprouts.

"At the store, I couldn't decide between cherry and orange sauce for the duck, so I bought ingredients for both. Now, it's cherries jubilee for dessert. Probably not as good as Cherry Garcia, but I'll put a lot of brandy in it. No one will mind."

"It all *smells* so wonderful." Grace put her handbag on the counter and smoothed her hair, inhaling the gamey aroma of roasting duck melding with the spicy smell of the sweet potatoes.

"Swirl this butter slowly into the sauce for me while I plate the smoked salmon."

"Three courses. So fancy, dearie. So organized."

"Don't worry. I'm really good at this. I could've been a celebrity chef," Zelda said with a straight face.

Acknowledging the joke, Grace removed her wire-rims and made a show of carefully polishing the thick lenses. "And I'm ready to be your spy."

Zelda slivered two lemons and arranged the slices on the salmon.

Just then Nick rushed into the kitchen. He decanted the wine while talking a mile a minute to Grace and Zelda.

"I'm going to have a quick shower. Down in a minute." He blew them a kiss on his way upstairs.

"He's very nervous. Either that or on cocaine." Grace pushed her glasses up on the bridge of her nose and popped a crispy Brussels sprout into her mouth.

"Grace!"

At that moment Eli and Ann arrived, followed almost immediately by the Duncans. Lourdes ushered them into the kitchen. Zelda pulled off her apron and greeted them.

Brooke wore a backless black jumpsuit with a bright red scarf and wild Christian Louboutins on her feet. Her short nails were painted such a dark red they were almost mahogany.

When Nick returned, refreshed from his shower, he barely said hello to Eli and Ann before making a beeline for Brooke. Grace and Zelda were too far away to hear what he said, but Brooke licked her lips in what appeared to be a lascivious fashion. Grace furtively elbowed Zelda, and Zelda whispered to her, "Spies don't do that."

"This one does."

There was an agitated atmosphere, which didn't relax, even with generous quantities of wine. At the end of the evening, Grace said, "Nick, the wine was too good. I'm afraid I'll have to ask Eli to drive me home. Zelda, I'll Uber here in the morning to get my car and have coffee with you, if that works."

"Good idea. Anytime is fine."

A bit later, while Zelda was still in the kitchen, a text came from Grace, "Still collecting data. Cover not blown."

Zelda texted back, "Full report anticipated."

By ten o'clock the following morning Zelda and Grace were curled up on the living room sofa with large mugs of cappuccino.

Grace reported, "In the car going home, Ann said she was confused by the relationship between the Blairs and the Duncans. I asked her to explain, but she just said there was a lot of what she thought was 'innuendo' flying around. Not sure what she meant by that and was not in a position to quiz her at the time."

"What did Eli say?"

"Nothing at all. It was foggy, and he was driving very carefully as I don't think he could've passed a Breathalyzer test last night."

"I didn't notice that he'd had too much to drink."

"Eli has admirable self-control, even when under the influence."

"You should've driven."

"I was in worse shape than he was." Grace held the back of her hand to her forehead. "Can you get me an aspirin?"

"Of course. I'll be right back. I really want to hear what you thought about Brooke."

After swallowing two tablets, Grace said, "In my opinion, Nick's car was parked near Brooke's house the other day because he was visiting her."

"I *knew* it. But I didn't want to know."

"Knowledge is power, dearie."

"In this case it's also sad and hurtful on so many counts."

"I know it is, but you don't have to act on it now. Or ever. But it's always good to know what's going on behind your back."

"I waver between indignation and bitterness, wanting to confront them and wanting to hide."

"This may burn out quickly." Grace finished the glass of water and put it on the table.

"Knowing Brooke like I do, I think she'll stick with Stuart. His bonus was double Nick's. She does the math."

"And Nick would be diminished in her eyes, reduced by alimony and child support. So if she's actually doing the math, this'll be short-lived."

"Stuart would be paying her, though…."

"What's important is how *you* feel."

"Numb. I feel numb. I know you won't believe this, but Nick's a good father."

"I'll take your word for it, but it *is* hard to believe."

Zelda's phone rang. "Brooke, let me call you back. Grace is here."

"Speak of the devil." Grace got up to leave. "I feel somewhat better now, and I promised Ann lunch in the faculty dining room. I'll try to find out what she meant by 'innuendo'. See you later in the week."

"How about a post-prandial call?"

"You're a tough spymaster."

That afternoon Zelda washed her hair with lavender shampoo and was about to attack it with the dryer when her phone rang.

"Ann really liked your duck, dearie. I had a lot of trouble getting her to define 'innuendo' in relation to you Blairs and the Duncans. She was much more interested in how good the orange sauce was with the sweet potatoes."

"So what did you get?"

"She said she *felt* it was a complicated situation. When I pushed her, she expounded on the complexities of office friendships where loyalty and ambition are at odds."

"And?"

"She thinks Nick might be up to something and that Stuart is smarter than Nick thinks he is. And that Brooke is a fool."

"A fool, how?"

"Ann thought Brooke was playing footsy with Nick last night. Ann said if she thought this, probably unspecified others might think this, too."

"Footsy at my dinner table?"

"According to my source."

"This really brings it home. Now *I* feel complicated. Nick is *my* husband. The father of *my* children. I don't want to be a single mother. I don't want to be the first in my family to be divorced. I want to keep my family together." The pitch of Zelda's voice became higher and higher.

"Deep breath, dearie. Do you want me to come over for a cup of tea?"

"How soon can you get here?"

"Forty-five minutes."

"Hurry."

# Chapter Thrirteen

The rain was steady that afternoon, and it was over an hour later before Grace arrived, dripping from the short sprint up the Blair's steep steps, red hair frizzing wildly.

Zelda had been standing at the window and rushed to open the door before Grace rang. "I'm so glad to see you." Against the instincts of both women, Grace held her strong arms wide, and Zelda allowed herself to fall into them.

Breaking away and leading Grace to the living room, Zelda said, "I've had a chance to think. I'm going to try to get Nick to ask for a transfer back to New York. Things will be better there."

"Geographic cures rarely work, but it's worth a try."

They settled into a low sofa facing away from the rain. The apricot-colored walls were cheerful on a day like this.

"What do you mean?"

"You'll have the same problems, just at a different address."

"Brooke won't be there."

"There are plenty of Brookes and only one Zelda."

"Do you think Nick knows that?"

"I don't know. But I *do* know you're the one responsible for keeping yourself and your children safe."

Zelda sucked in her breath. "Safe. Of course you're right. I'd never thought about my responsibility in this other than to keep the marriage together and not tell a soul. Now that you and Hank knows, it looks different to me."

"Keep your pencil sharp, dearie."

Lourdes brought a tray, and while the women were sipping tea, Zelda's cell rang. She looked down and saw it was from Phoebe's school. "I've got to take this, Grace."

After a few pleasantries and a long pause, Zelda said, "Yes, Miss Adkins. I'll see you tomorrow morning at eight."

Zelda felt her blood drain from her face and turned to Grace. "Oh my God! Phoebe's using kickboxing moves on other kids. Acting out. Not hurting them, but…she must've seen…"

Zelda's mind raced, replaying recent attacks. Her mind settled on the morning of the Fourth of July. She was brushing her teeth. Phoebe could have peeked in. It must have been then, she thought.

Grace was very matter-of-fact. "I can ask around and find out the best child psychologists in the area, if you want."

"I want. And no matter what you say about geography, I'm going back to New York."

"How are you going to deal with your parents?"

"I don't know, but we'll be safer there. All this started out here."

"It's Nick, not San Francisco."

"He'll change when he gets home."

"I hope so. But consider leaving the suitcase at my house, just in case."

"I can't think about that now, but it's probably a good idea. I'm not going to tell Nick anything tonight. I'll wait 'til I've seen the teacher."

"Very sensible."

"Please stay for supper. I can't face it alone."

"Of course I'll stay."

The rain had stopped by the time Grace left the Blairs, but a sharp stab of loneliness hit her as she was driving home to Woodside. The moon and stars were exceptionally bright in the clear winter sky guaranteeing that tomorrow would be crisp and sunny, just as she liked it. She'd begun to feel fond of Zelda and was sad thinking of her returning to New York, but since Zelda seemed to be determined to save her marriage, Grace had reluctantly agreed that the move back east was an obvious first step.

The evening had been awkward. Zelda told Nick she'd been asked to go to the school the next day, elaborately explaining that she thought they wanted her help with the book fair, maybe even to chair it. What did Nick think? And on and on about book fair possibilities.

Then in an effort to appear totally relaxed, Zelda had a bit too much wine and started voicing concerns that maybe the appointment at the school was not about the book fair, but something more serious, like anti-social behavior. What did Nick think about that? Shouldn't the school be supportive of their students? And on and on about anti-social behavior.

Grace escaped as soon as she could after supper. She was exhausted and relieved when she finally turned into her driveway. Her phone pinged as she opened the door.

Zelda had written: Can you believe it? Nick and I finished the bottle. Probably Eli's fault—his favorite wine. It's a good one, though, so maybe no hangover.

Grace replied: 2 aspirin and sweet dreams will fix you up.

Zelda's response: I'll dream of Eli.

"Oh, God," Grace said aloud to her empty house.

The next day dawned as expected, and Grace started it off with a slow jog around the track in a wooded area near her house. She held her gaze at the horizon as she ran at a steady pace, appreciating the cloudless blue expanse before her and the wonderful smell of pine all around.

She had to consciously remind herself that this was not such a glorious day for Zelda, and when she returned, she called and left a message. "I hope your meeting with the teacher went well. I'll ask around the faculty lounge for the right psychologist and call you later."

Several hours later, she reached Zelda's voicemail again. This time Grace said, "There's a Miss Shook who's very young but has had impressive success with children. I'll text you her contact info."

The call came from Zelda almost immediately. "It's worse than I thought."

"Tell me."

"During supervised play, Phoebe always wants to be the father of the family."

"And?"

"Well, she kicks the mother. Not hard, but naturally, the school doesn't like this sort of thing and wants her to see a shrink. I'll call that Miss Shook this afternoon. Hope I don't have to be the one to give Nick the details."

"Won't he be furious if it comes from a third party?"

"I think it's prudent. He'd have time to process the info in front of a pro."

"You're probably right. Call her now and say you have to see her this evening. This can't wait."

"Miss Adkins said the same thing. We should go as soon as possible and set a course of therapy for Phoebe. She gave me the names of several people, but I want to go to Miss Shook. And I'm glad to hear she's young."

"Make the call, dearie."

Zelda pressed the numbers, explained the situation to the psychologist and was able to get a six o'clock appointment that evening.

She called Grace back. "Now what?"

"Call Nick."

She put Grace on hold and got Nick on the phone. "The school wants us to go to a psychologist right away to talk about Phoebe and make appointments for her to start therapy."

"What a load of shit. Phoebe doesn't need therapy."

Zelda dove right in. "She's been play-acting father of the family, and she kicks the mother."

"I see."

"Our appointment is at six. I'll text you the address."

"I'll be there."

Zelda recounted the conversation, and Grace responded, "See? That wasn't so bad."

Zelda arrived for the appointment five minutes before six and found Nick already seated in the waiting room. Miss Shook turned out to be a tall, skinny brunette column of chic with a welcoming smile and firm handshake.

During the hour session, the cards were placed on the table, and though Nick didn't actually apologize to Zelda, he seemed appropriately cowed. Zelda appreciated this and decided not to bring up the subject of his suspected affair with Brooke. She figured there'd been enough shock for one day.

Conflicting thoughts roamed around Zelda's head all evening until finally she decided not to make any changes at all. She called Grace and said, "Miss Shook is perfect, and Phoebe's going to love her. Now I'm thinking we shouldn't go back to New York. My gut says we all need to stay right here and get the Miss Shook treatment."

"This *is* good news. I'm going to celebrate with some Rocky Road. Did you drop the Brooke bomb?"

"I'm going to see the shrink alone next week and will do it then."

"Tell me more about her."

"She said all her friends call her Shookie, and Phoebe should call her Miss Shookie. She is gorgeous, warm and friendly."

"I'm glad this came to a head so you have a professional to talk to."

"I would've never gone to one otherwise."

"Selfishly, I'm pleased you're staying in San Francisco."

"At least for now. So much has happened lately, I need to catch my breath."

"How's Nick taking it?"

"He's acting exactly like nothing happened. He made a point of putting the kids to bed tonight, overseeing brushing teeth, et cetera. Very jolly and overly animated. He's in his study now with the door closed."

"Guess you'll be getting the silent treatment."

"Definitely. We left Shookie's in separate cars. Nick got home before me, so we haven't talked yet."

"You'll have to discuss it."

"Neither one of us wants to. Maybe it'll all have to take place in Shookie's office."

"She'll guide you. But you have to do what *you* feel is right."

"I feel nothing at all. I'm numb. Completely numb."

"You've got to move on from 'numb' and introduce yourself to your feelings, dearie. It's very healthy to recognize them and call them by name."

"Are you the shrink now?"

"No, but I know there's always something interesting underneath numb."

# Chapter Fourteen

The month that followed was without incident. In fact, the lack of incident was what made it strange. Nick and Zelda were very polite to each other, and Nick brought flowers home several times. They continued to see the same friends, and on the surface nothing was amiss. But they never discussed why Phoebe was seeing Shookie twice a week or that they were seeing her separately as well.

Hank was having a hard time getting in touch with Zelda, and the few times they talked the conversations had no content, Zelda adroitly evading all questions. This went on for weeks and finally Hank called Grace. After he introduced himself, Grace made no pretense of bothering with small talk saying, "Zelda's shutting me out."

"Me, too." Hank admitted.

"If I hadn't heard such rave reviews about Miss Shook, the shrink, I'd go over to Pierce Street right now and make a nuisance of myself. But I'm sure Zelda's in good hands."

Hank replied, "She's taken to calling me when she knows I can't pick up and leaves cheery little messages. If I didn't know better, I'd think she was living inside some sort of pink cloud."

"I'm getting the same treatment. Rainbows and unicorns."

"Maybe I should come out there."

"You could stay with me, but I live in the sticks. You'd have to rent a car."

"Thanks, but I'll stay with Zelda. Let me check when I can get away. Do you think I could see the shrink?"

"No. That would never fly."

"Quite right, too, but I'd like to give her my two cents."

"I know how you feel. I'd like to give her mine as well." Grace asked him to keep her apprised of his travel plans. "Looking forward to meeting you, Henry James O'Neil."

That same day, as Zelda was leaving Shookie's, she ran into the enviable and elusive Donna Hall in the waiting room. Neither woman could hide her surprise. Both appeared delighted by this coincidence and checked their phones for availability, making plans for lunch the following day.

They met at Battery, both arriving five minutes before the appointed hour. Zelda always arrived early. She'd much rather wait for someone than have the stress of knowing someone was waiting for her. Kevin O'Neil had made sure his children knew his view that being late was tantamount to stealing. Stealing time, which could never be paid back. O'Neils were on time.

Neither of them mentioned Shookie during lunch, although Zelda was dying to know what brought the sensational and single Donna to the door of a psychologist specializing in children's issues.

Not wanting to discuss personal matters, Zelda steered the conversation to the safety of the literature sector but noticed Donna kept an eye on her watch. When coffee was served, Donna said, "I'm sorry, but I have to run. I've got a golf lesson at Burlingame. I have to change and get there by three-thirty."

"Our Jane Austen lecturer plays there, too. Do you know her?"

"Grace was in my mother's class at Vassar, so I've known her, though not well, ever since she came to Stanford, which is to say, most of my life. She's a real character and brilliant in her field."

"I've only gotten to know her recently, but I'm devoted to her."

"We'll have to have lunch with her one day."

Donna dashed off, but Zelda was pleased. They'd had a nice enough time and the half-promised future lunch seemed probable. Zelda still had no idea what Donna was doing at Shookie's but not bad for round one, she thought.

Once in her car, Zelda got Grace on the phone. "I didn't know you've known Donna Hall most of her life."

"So now you do, dearie. She's as bright as she's pretty. And a very nice girl."

"I didn't notice that you knew her so well at Brooke's."

"Your attention was elsewhere, if I remember correctly."

Zelda felt blood rush to her face. "Let's all get together. I'd love to know her better."

"One of these days, I'm going to find a reason for having a party for all my friends who are half my age and under. It'll be a blast."

"I'll make that list for you, starting with Donna."

"Okay. The list is due before spring vacay starts at Stanford. I might find time during the break."

Zelda emailed reasons for Grace to throw a party. Near the top was, "Hank's coming to SF for ten days."

Grace emailed right back: "The party starts on day two of Hank's stay at seven and will continue the whole time he's here. Who could possibly resist Henry James O'Neil?"

"How did you know he's Henry James?"

"You told me."

"Good memory. We accept your invitation with great pleasure. Need any help?"

"No, but thanks."

Grace hadn't given a party in ages, but she hadn't forgotten how. It would be a seventies theme, she decided. She had plenty of party clothes left over from that era, and they still fit.

She planned a Polynesian disco buffet complete with strobe lights and lava lamps, a DJ and a bartender specializing in umbrella drinks.

The guest list grew and grew, and suddenly Grace had to include those in their forties as well, so as not to hurt any feelings. Soon it became apparent that her house was too small. A tent would have to be pitched, and somehow the pool would have to become a dance floor. Hang the expense, she thought, and sold some stock she didn't need.

The night of the party was cool and clear. Everyone invited turned up. They came in a variety of costumes, heavy on the hot pants for the slender and a full complement of wigs and unusual accessories for the others.

Brooke wore the hottest pants of all, black sequins with fishnets and platform shoes. No one in the seventies ever looked so good. Grace noticed Stuart watched her with pride as she prowled the tent for exotic prey, diamonds glinting through her long dark hair in the strobe lighting.

What happened that night was unexpected. Not only did Brooke and Stuart appear to be the happy couple, but Nick, who rarely drank to excess, overdid it, and fell while dancing with Grace.

Zelda noticed Donna and Hank were struck by each other. It was fascination at first sight, and they spent the whole evening together.

Eli was nowhere to be seen. Zelda searched for him and finally asked Grace where he was hiding.

"He's in Connecticut. His mother had elective surgery, and he's there supervising her recovery."

Covering up her extreme disappointment, Zelda babbled, "Elective surgery? Why would she do that? Who would elect surgery?"

"I'm sure she had a good reason, and I don't like to pry," Grace replied.

"I hope it's not a facelift. She's perfect as is. She should be landmarked or something. Why would Eli go?"

"Dearie, Eli has romantic feelings for you, and as you are a married woman with four children, striving to save her marriage, I think he might be trying to avoid acquiring more feelings of that nature."

"But I have those feelings for him, too."

"You have to put your family first. You told me so yourself."

Zelda sighed. "That's right. I do, but can't we be close friends?"

"I have some experience in this field, and I would say it is unlikely to be successful."

"How long is he going to be in Connecticut?"

"He'll be back when classes start."

Out of the blue, Zelda said, "I wonder what got into Nick tonight."

"Don't let him drive."

Just then Nick came up to Grace and Zelda. "Where's Eli? I have a great deal to offer him. I'll get him in at ground zero, and he'll make a fortune."

"What's the deal? Maybe I want in." Grace forced a smile.

"Only for players. Sorry, professor. Can't even tell you what it is."

Grace took a sip of her drink and eyed him skeptically. "Keep me in mind for something less mysterious."

Zelda went off and danced with Nick who did not seem to be noticing Brooke. Not pointedly not noticing, but actually not noticing. Odd, Grace observed.

Later on Zelda found Grace again. "I hope I'm not the real reason Eli's missing this epic party."

"But you are."

"I feel his absence tonight like a weight. I feel like I'm wearing one of those lead X-Ray blankets they put on you at the dentist's office. I was so looking forward to seeing him. I haven't seen him since the night of the Alexis Cabernet Sauvignon."

"Yes, six weeks, but who's counting?"

"Was Eli counting?"

"What do you think?"

Zelda's voice dropped to a whisper. "I don't know what to think."

"I don't either. But I have great compassion for both of you."

It would have been too cruel to drag Hank away from Donna, so Zelda told him she'd leave a key under the mat. The valet brought Nick's black BMW, and Zelda got into the driver's seat.

A thin drizzle was beginning to mist the windshield, and the hypnotic swish of the wipers put Nick straight to sleep. Zelda ached with loneliness as she drove through the moonless night towards the city, the car a glowing orb slicing through the darkness.

# Chapter Fifteen

The next morning, Zelda had breakfast with the children and saw them off. She was barefoot, wearing her white terrycloth robe, and perusing the newspaper at the kitchen table when the phone rang. It was Brooke.

"I have to start planning the May meeting of the book club, and I need your help."

"My help?" Zelda questioned.

"I want to do something totally different."

"Totally different." Zelda repeated like someone in a trance.

"What's the *matter* with you, Zelda? You sound like you're smoking crack."

Zelda shook herself like a dog getting out of a lake. "I'm just tired. We got home after midnight. And you were still at the party."

"Get some coffee and listen to me."

Zelda looked down at her half-drunk cup. "I'm listening."

"The meeting will start at nine-thirty. I'll have Patrick do something very modern, bare branches and things."

"Hmmm."

"We'll set up the living room like the fall meeting and have Grace *et al.* in front. I suppose Eli will be coming."

"Hmmm."

"At the end of their thing, I'll make a speech saying how much we loved reading Jane two hundred years after she wrote and that I imagine a hundred years from now people will still be enjoying her books."

"Sounds good." Trance-like moved on to bored.

"Then we'll go into the dining room for coffee. I'm going to take everything off the walls and have a light show going on with creepy music. What do you think?"

"How do you come up with these ideas, Brooke?"

"I stay up late and get up early. You know that. And the food will be silver, stark white and black."

"Silver?"

"You know those almonds? And silver-leaf covering little cakes."

"I don't know, but I'll believe you. Very twenty-second century." Zelda slugged back her lukewarm coffee.

"It'll be chic as Hell." Brooke sounded exultant.

"Inviting the press?"

"Of course not. I saw your brother was getting to know our Donna last night."

"I haven't seen him yet this morning." Zelda combed her fingers through her thick auburn hair, sticking a pencil in it to keep it off her neck.

"Maybe he had a sleepover at Donna's."

"I sincerely doubt it."

Brooke changed the subject back to something more interesting to her. "Maybe I'll give the chair of the book club back to Donna. Liane says I have better opportunities coming up."

"You did a stellar job this year. Everyone says so."

"They do? Like who?"

"Like everyone, Brooke. You must know that."

"I like hearing it from you. I've got to go."

"What do you need my help with?"

"Nothing really. I only wanted your opinion on my plans."

"Go, Brooke, go."

"Let's have lunch next week. I haven't seen you in ages."

"Hank's here."

"He can come, too."

"Are you kidding?"

"Forget Hank, then. He'll be glad to get rid of you for a couple of hours. I'll call you when I see how my week is shaping up."

"Right." Zelda tapped "end" but kept the phone in her hand and called Grace.

Grace answered sleepily. Zelda looked at her watch. "I hope I didn't wake you up."

"No, the goddamn sun did that for you. It decided to make one of its rare appearances on the one day I want to sleep."

"It was a great party."

"I know. Even I had a good time."

"What do you mean, 'even I'?"

"Oh, you know." Grace sounded sad. "I was disappointed Eli wasn't there."

"Do you blame me for that?"

"No, of course not. I rely on him too much. I know that. Anyway, I felt lost without him."

"Well, you weren't. By the way, Grace, Brooke's planning the May meeting."

"You won't believe this, but she told me that she had to check with her astrologer for a date and get back to me."

"That's how it works with Brooke. I figure the astrologer told her to stick to Stuart. Did you notice them last night?"

"I did, and I noticed that Nick couldn't care less. We might've been wrong in suspecting them." Grace yawned.

"When I talked to Shookie about my assumptions, she was non-committal, but I got the impression she didn't think anything had happened." Zelda inspected her toenails and made a mental note to book a pedicure.

"How's Phoebe at school these days." Grace was beginning to sound alert.

"No further incidents that I know of."

"And you? Any incidents?"

"None." Zelda poured more coffee in her cup.

"Shookie was a good choice. Have you and Nick talked much about it?"

"We barely talk. He's been acting sort of jumpy lately. Wait, I hear Hank coming downstairs. I'll call you later."

"Bring him for lunch. I have tons of leftovers."

"Good idea. We'll be there at noon."

"Shall I invite Donna?" Grace's voice was full of drama.

"By all means."

"It's a disaster zone here. We'll eat in the tent. They aren't coming 'til tomorrow to take it down."

Hank stumbled in, looking ridiculous, wearing Zelda's short blue satin robe. "Who's that you're talking to so early in the morning?"

"It's nine here. Noon in New York. Do you want an aspirin?"

"I'm fine. I really like your friend Donna."

"Everyone noticed. She'll be at Grace's for lunch today. Just the four of us."

"Brilliant and beautiful. Why didn't you introduce her to me before?"

"I really don't know her that well."

"She said you had lunch with her the other day."

"It was a first."

"Let's talk about you and Nick and Phoebe."

"Let's not." Zelda handed him a steaming mug of Earl Grey with milk and honey. "Get dressed, and we'll go for a jog. These hills give you a real workout."

"You'll have to make some decisions."

"I know, but not this morning. And things are neutral now. Shookie has staunched the bleeding." Zelda tried to sound casual, but she was beginning to panic. The conversation was going too deep.

"That's not enough."

"It's enough for now. Do you get the feeling I don't want to discuss this?" Zelda's lips tightened, her voice steely.

"I'll get dressed."

They ran hard for forty minutes and came home elated by endorphins. "I'm so glad you're here, Hanky. Forgive me if I was grumpy this morning."

"I'm your big brother. You can be yourself. Anyway, I like you grumpy. Grumpy reminds me of the good old days."

They ate toast and drank tea while they chatted about their siblings. Zelda made sure the talk was centered on others. Then suddenly she said, "Look at the time! We'd better shower and get on the road. Don't want to keep Donna waiting."

"Definitely not." Hank got up. "And don't call me Hanky in front of her. You know I hate that."

"I love it, though. And Mom always refers to you as Hanky."

"I can't get through to her. But, you. You can stop." Hank started up the stairs.

"Okay, you win, Hanky Doodle."

Looking back over his shoulder, he replied, "God, Zelda. *Grow up.*"

In the car going to Grace's, Zelda reached out and touched Hank's hand. "Grace thinks I should go back to college and get my BA."

"I can't believe you haven't done that already. How many credits are you missing?"

"Quite a few, but I can start with summer school and go on for as long as it takes. No more than two courses per semester."

"What are you thinking of as a career?" Hank peered at Zelda.

"I don't know. I'm not really good at anything."

"Don't say that. You're wonderful with people. What about studying psychology? Get a BS instead. Since you're so full of it, maybe you already have one."

"I'll ignore the scatological slur and admit I've never thought of that before. One thing's for sure, I look forward to the Shookie sessions every week."

"Well, change your major and give her some competition, Zelly Belly."

"Do you think I could?"

"I think you'd be good, really good."

"I'm psyched! It'll take years, but I'm sure I would *love* it."

Her enthusiasm was bubbling over as she drove up to Grace's, flattening out considerably when she saw Donna's silver Lexus parked in front. She was embarrassed she didn't have a college degree and wouldn't want the book club group to know. She had a reputation to protect, after all. Everyone thought she was brilliant on the subject of American Literature, assuming she was highly educated, and she was going to keep it that way.

"For God's sake, Hanky, don't mention that I'm a college drop-out to Donna. And I won't call you Hanky. Promise."

"Okay, but one slip, and you're dead meat."

"Got it."

Zelda parked next to Donna and strolled into the tent. It looked so sad and lonely without the flashing lights and thrumming beat roaring on. Abandoned now, with no sign of Donna or Grace.

"Let's try the house."

They found Grace and Donna decorating platters of Polynesian fare with paper umbrellas and pineapple cut outs.

Grace looked up. "Hi, kids. Just in time to pitch in. Hank, will you put some rum in that pitcher of punch? And, Zelda, do something about this pork. It has no taste. Donna and I were just talking about you two."

"Grace! How can you say such things?" Donna was visibly flustered.

"Well, dearie, we weren't saying salacious things. Only sweet things. We'll save the rough stuff for later. I've put knives and forks on one of the tables in the tent. Let's go in there and eat."

Spirited conversations lasted well into the afternoon. Finally, Zelda said, "I've got kids to see. Hank, why don't you stay and drive back with Donna?"

Grace agreed. "Yes, do stay, Hank, so we can discuss Zelda's character defects behind her back."

"How could a brother resist?"

On the drive back, Zelda considered the two dinner parties she and Nick would be giving in April, mostly to entertain valued Silverman clients, but a few prospects would be included, as well. Nick had put Eli on both guest lists. If she'd asked herself how she felt about this, she would've admitted to a stinging swarm of confusing, conflicting feelings. But rather than chase self-reflection, she concentrated on composing the menus, deadening the pain with thoughts of taste, texture and color combinations.

Hank and Donna stayed at Grace's until it was almost dark. While driving back to San Francisco, they phoned and made a reservation at Garibaldi, a small Italian restaurant near Donna's apartment, and by the time Donna dropped Hank off on Pierce Street, the big house was dark and silent, looming over the steep hill.

# Chapter Sixteen

Zelda tossed and turned all night, wondering whether to invite Eli to the Silverman parties. At dawn, she fell into a deep sleep, not waking until ten. Looking at the clock, at first she felt guilty, then amazed. Not one person, on this Sunday morning, had hammered on her door. How odd, she thought.

Outside her window, San Francisco was shrouded in mist, which was turning slowly into dense fog, softening the sounds of the city and adding to the eerie quiet. She put on a kimono and wandered downstairs, surprised to find herself alone.

In the kitchen, there were signs of hastily eaten breakfasts and a note from Nick saying he and Hank were entertaining the children. They'd taken her car and would be back after lunch. He said she should take it easy but not forget to get started on the April dinners. So she typed up the menus and a to-do list, determined not to think about whether or not to include Eli.

Wallowing in the luxury of having the house to herself, she drifted from room to room doing standing stretches, admiring the house and making notes on her phone of what needed refurbishing. Finally, she hurried upstairs and pulled on jeans and a gray sweatshirt. Surveying herself in the wall of mirrors, she tore off the sweatshirt and replaced it with a burnt orange silk shirt, one Nick had brought back from Hong Kong. Much better, she thought.

A text came in from Hank saying Donna had joined them for a picnic and could Zelda please include her in whatever plans they had for the evening.

Zelda texted back: "We're home with the kids tonight, but I'll grant you a dispensation."

Hank got right back, "Dispensation unnecessary. Donna wants to join us in the kitchen. Back soon."

"Damn," Zelda said under her breath, "this is *not* how I imagined getting to know Donna. Hanky takes everything I want." She laughed out loud at her childishness.

The evening was relaxed, but Zelda noticed Nick checking his phone more than usual. She might take a look at that phone if a safe moment presented itself. Remembering she could've looked last night while Nick was sleeping, her first thought was how foolish to have passed up a golden opportunity, immediately replaced by thinking, "What a rotten person I'm becoming."

After the kids were tucked in, Donna and Hank departed for a drink at the Top of the Mark, and Nick scurried to his study, leaving Zelda free to call Grace.

Zelda was pouring hot water over a teabag when Grace answered. She started right in. "Just so you know, I'm morally degrading with age."

"Most people do, dearie. Anything the authorities need to be aware of?"

"I want to examine Nick's phone."

"Shows you're practical and thrifty, saving on private detectives."

"You think I should?" Zelda's voice was an octave higher than normal as she placed the kettle back on the burner.

"I can't condone such frightful behavior, but I might possibly do such a thing myself."

"Your standards are very low, professor."

"My road is higher than yours. I, 'might possibly' and you, 'want to examine'."

"I know. Terrible. And my Uncle Chris is a priest." Zelda pried the top off a jar and trickled honey into her cup.

"Make no questionable ethical decisions, but stay alert for your chance."

"You're a bad influence on the young."

"Possibly."

"I don't know what I'd do without you."

"You don't have to. Sleep tight."

Zelda thought how lucky she was to have Grace in her time zone and knocked on the door of Nick's study. "Do you want anything before I go up?"

"I'm fine, thanks. Won't be long."

Walking into her room, Zelda couldn't believe her eyes. There was Nick's phone, charging on his bedside table. Without thinking twice she sprinted to it, pressed the password and opened messages. She scrolled and scrolled but didn't see Brooke's name. Nothing in recent calls, either. Searching contacts, she found Brooke's cell number and a note with the girls' names.

Zelda plugged it back in, called Grace and ducked into her dressing room. "The phone's clean," she whispered.

"Well, we're either wrong, or he's taking precautions."

"Nick would *never* suspect me of spying." Zelda was indignant.

"Little does he know you. But he might be extra careful because of Stuart."

"He's coming upstairs. Call you tomorrow." Zelda hit "end".

Nick picked up his phone, kissed Zelda goodnight and returned to his study, phone in hand.

Alone in her bed, Zelda wanted to conjure up a dream of herself and Eli, but the vision wouldn't come. She acknowledged she really didn't know him. There were layers and layers of undiscovered territory underneath his handsome exterior, and all she could think about were his efforts not to see her. She was too tired to dwell on this depressing thought for long, and hanging on to what Grace said about his romantic feelings for her, she floated off to sleep.

The next morning, Nick had left for the office, and Hank had finished breakfast before Zelda came downstairs. She said to Hank, "I've got a school thing and Shookie today, but otherwise, I'm all yours. Did you make plans with Donna?"

"I'm going to take her out to dinner. Okay if I tag along to school and Shookie?"

"Sure. I know Phoebe would be wowed to have her Uncle Hank at the recital. And Shookie's easygoing. If we show up together, then she can either let you come to the session, or you can wait. It's only fifty minutes."

"Do we have time for a run?"

"Let me change my shoes."

While they were jogging in Alta Plaza, Hank said, "Is everything okay with Nick's business?"

"Of course. Why?"

"I heard him yelling at someone on the phone last night. A little after midnight. The door to his study was closed. No idea what he was saying, but thought you should know."

"Midnight is too late to bully people in San Francisco and way too late to even whisper to people on the east coast. I don't know what time that would make it in Hong Kong, but he does a lot of business there."

"He was out of control. Maybe you should mention this to Shookie."

"Maybe."

As it turned out, Shookie let Zelda decide if she wanted Hank in the session or not, and it was Zelda who brought up Nick's midnight conversation.

"My brother overheard an angry conversation last night."

Hank interrupted. "I may have minimized this to Zelda. What I heard was incandescent rage, all but shaking the door off its hinges." Shookie listened, but said nothing.

At school, Phoebe was all over her uncle and dragged him around, pointing up at him and saying, "He's my Uncle Hanky." Hank smiled and twiddled his eyebrows in Zelda's direction. She just shrugged and talked to the other mothers until it was time to go.

Nick was home when they arrived and asked Zelda how the dinner party plans were coming along and if Eli would be attending one or both. Zelda hadn't been aware of making up her mind about Eli, but she lied smoothly. "He's not going to be in town. Something about his mother having an operation."

"Damn. Let me have a look at the menus."

Zelda printed out copies as well as the guest list with notes on who had accepted. As she handed them to Nick, she caught Hank's eye.

"Good job, Zelda. Very well thought out," Nick muttered. "And I like the menus, all except the pheasant. That's an autumn dish. Have lamb instead."

Nick pleaded pressing work and sequestered himself in his study. Zelda slumped down in a chair near the printer and said, "You may not think so, but that was an A+ from Nick. I've never had such high praise."

"Why don't you let Nick get on with whatever he's working on and come out to dinner with Donna and me tonight. I'd love to have two beautiful women at my table."

"Where exactly is that table?"

"Some place called Boulevard that Donna said was good."

"I haven't been. If you're sure you don't mind, I'd love to go."

"I'm here because of you, not her. This time, at least."

"Planning on coming back soon?"

"You never know. I'll sit with the kids while they have supper, and you can put your feet up before we go."

Nick chose to go with them, but he was distracted and clamped a damper on the evening. Though they got home early, Zelda was exhausted from the effort she'd made to jolly Nick along for Donna and Hank's sake.

Tired though she was, Zelda lay awake for a long time. Her mind was full of Eli Russell again. She could picture him, bright blue eyes, short graying hair, athletic body. But try as she might, she couldn't quite imagine herself standing next to him.

# Chapter Seventeen

The Blair's two dinner parties in April were topnotch, although Zelda's heart wasn't in them. Brooke said to Stuart on the way home from the first one, "Zelda's catching on."

"Zelda's good, but you're ten times better, and I have a little surprise for you this weekend." Stuart took his eyes off the road and looked across at Brooke.

"Yes?"

"We have an appointment with a real estate agent in Tahoe."

"Oh, my God, I love you so much, Stuart. You don't know how much this means to me. And the girls. We're going to have the best summer ever."

After the second party, Brooke said to Stuart, "What's *wrong* with that Zelda? I caught her yawning at the table."

"She'll never have your focus and energy."

"She should know how to do her job by now." Brooke sounded cross.

"Nick told me she's going to take some courses this summer."

"Probably working on her PhD in American Lit, for all the good it'll do her, if she can't stay awake at her own dinner table."

"Who wants to discuss books, anyway?"

"God, Stuart, I love that you don't give a damn what people think of your intellectual refinements."

"Why would I? I can buy 'em and sell 'em, those literature people. Why do *you* care so much?"

"I just do. I want to show people like Donna Hall that she's not the only one who can read a book."

"Jeez. Women." Stuart paused and said, "I hope you're not going to fill the house in Tahoe with professors and idiots like that."

"Come on, Stuart. Professors by definition are not idiots."

"I want some guests who know how to have fun."

"You deserve to have exactly what you want. Don't worry. No professors. Just Silverman cronies, if you want."

"My Brooke's the bomb."

The morning after the second dinner, the Blair children had already left for their activities, and Zelda was alone at the kitchen table when Nick came in. The speed and force of his kick to the table was impressive, but it was the noise of china and glass breaking that registered first with Zelda. She looked up at him in shock.

"So, you think it's okay to yawn in the face of my best client?" Nick stamped on the shards and kicked Zelda's chair hard.

"What?"

"Stuart just called and told me what happened."

"What happened?"

Nick stamped again, ground slivers of glass under his heel and left the house, slamming the front door furiously.

Once Zelda could speak, she called Grace whose phone went directly to voicemail. She checked the time and called her mother. Abigail answered on the first ring. "Mom—" was all Zelda could get out before her hysterical sobbing started.

Eventually, Abigail got Zelda calmed down and suggested she go see Shookie. If she weren't available, Abigail directed Zelda to drive to Stanford and wait in Grace's office.

Shookie was with a patient. Zelda got in her car and headed for Stanford, leaving a message for Grace that she was on her way.

When Zelda arrived, Grace was sitting bolt upright in her hard desk chair. She got up and hugged the younger woman, muttering soothing sounds. Zelda recounted her tale disjointedly but was able to listen closely to Grace.

"Go to my house now. My housekeeper, Germaine, is there. No one is kinder or nicer than Germaine. She'll take care of you until I can get out of here. I won't be long. Have a bath and get into bed." Grace had spoken slowly and softly, as if to a child.

Germaine was ready with a cup of chicken broth, a hot bath already drawn and a crisp, white nightshirt laid on the turned-down bed in the blue guest room. Zelda moaned with relief.

"Professor Lloyd got through to Miss Shook," the housekeeper said. "She's cancelled her next two appointments and is on her way here."

By the time Shookie and Grace were seated on the bed with Zelda, she had already started defending Nick. She said she'd provoked him. It wasn't as dramatic as all that, she said, and really what she had to do was get home and clear up the broken bits before the children got there.

When Shookie and Grace objected, a spasm of irritation creased Zelda's forehead into a frown. She was annoyed that they wanted to make such a big deal out of this. "The children can't come home to broken pottery and glass all over the place. I have to go."

They couldn't argue with that. But Grace said, "You stay here. I'll do the cleaning up."

"No, please. I'm embarrassed I made such a fuss over nothing."

"This isn't nothing, Zelda." Shookie's voice was firm. "And your reaction now is indicative of trauma bonding."

"Look, it just wasn't all that bad. I exaggerated because I was tired."

The two women agreed upsetting Zelda further would be neither healthy nor productive. So Zelda called the shots and insisted on driving her car home. Grace followed her to Pierce Street, and they vacuumed the mess without speaking, both of them troubled and lost in thought.

Once the kitchen was back to normal, Zelda made tea and said, "It'll be safer if I let this go."

"Are you that afraid of Nick?"

"I'm not afraid of him. It's not that. There's a lot of pressure on him at Silverman. It won't happen again."

"Zelda, you're playing with fire. Open your eyes."

"I've got to call my mother and tell her I was overtired. It's going to be okay, Grace, really. Don't worry."

"I *am* worried. You have to come out of denial. It's like Stockholm syndrome or something."

"I have to do what I think is right. And for now, that is to make a quiet, loving home for my children. No more drama."

"You're not yourself, dearie. Please let me at least stay with you until Lourdes comes back."

"I'm fine, and you have a seminar at three. Please don't go on about this, but thank you for taking such good care of me."

As soon as Grace got in her car, she called Hank and recounted the events of the day. "Your sister's in shock and acting like a lunatic. She won't let me take charge which, of course, I should."

After discussing the saga, Hank said, "Speaking from a legal point of view, there's nothing any of us can do. And she would kill me if I told our dad. Mom might or might not tell him, but it's her call."

Abigail O'Neil allowed Zelda to convince her that nothing much had happened. Zelda claimed she was overtired, and Abigail wanted to believe her, so she did. Best not to mention this to Kevin, Abigail thought.

Hank called his mother. "I think this thing with Nick and Zelda is getting out of hand."

"Don't worry, Hanky. I talked to Zelda, and she sounded fine. She's just overtired – you know how she gets."

"She may be hiding the severity from you, Mom."

"I don't think so, and she said she didn't want Dad to know."

Hank heard the warning in his mother's voice, and as his other line was ringing, he replied, "Right. I've got to go. Let's talk later."

Zelda's teeth started chattering when she realized she was alone in the house, but she managed to drink a small tumbler of brandy and lie down for an hour. By sheer force of will, she completed the tasks she'd set for the day and even made a batch of chocolate chip cookies. Though still warm, they were ready in time for dessert.

Nick came home while Zelda and the children were still seated at the table. He poured a glass of milk and joined them, eating his share of the cookies. Since neither of the adults wanted to be alone together, they went their separate ways, Zelda to help Lourdes with the children's nighttime routine and Nick to his study.

Zelda didn't go back downstairs. She understood Nick wouldn't be coming to bed until she was asleep and looked on it as a courtesy.

In the middle of the night, Zelda awoke and registered that Nick was sleeping peacefully on his side of the bed. They'd successfully managed to avoid speaking directly to each other since the episode, and Zelda wanted to keep things that way as long as possible.

She heard Nick getting dressed early the next morning and feigned sleep until she was sure he'd left the house. She spent the day ferrying the children to and fro, thinking all the while that she wouldn't be able to bring herself to talk to any of her intimates.

She texted Shookie and canceled her appointment for that afternoon. By letting the calls from her mother, Grace and Hank go to voicemail, she got through the day.

If only they'd leave me alone, she thought. If only they'd let me put one foot in front of the other, I could find my balance. If only.

# Chapter Eighteen

A conference call, including Hank, Abigail and Grace, deter-mined the group would stay in touch with each other, but they would allow Zelda to isolate for as long as she wanted. Grace wasn't convinced this was the right action but went along with the others, accepting her non-family status with quiet dignity, but not enthusiasm.

Zelda continued to avoid contact with the others, and though she attended her Shookie sessions, she kept the focus on Phoebe. After two weeks, she resumed her frequent calls to her mother, keeping them brief, more like tweets than chats. The same kind of contact with Grace and Hank started shortly thereafter.

Calls from Brooke became more frequent as the May book club meeting approached. This time Brooke's concerns were more about whether Donna would ask her to continue as president or not.

"I thought you said your astrologer predicted better opportunities for you," Zelda commented.

"She was right. I'm chairing the hospital benefit next year."

"You'll be good at getting rich people to write fat checks."

"It's not for the prestige. I really want to help the hospital. You can be on my committee."

"It would be a waste since we'd pick the same pockets."

"Whatever, but I really love chairing the book club. And whether he'll admit it or not, Stuart's impressed. I like to keep him impressed. Is Nick impressed with you?"

"Nick's never been impressed with me. And if you don't mind my saying so, that's a weird relationship standard."

"If you want to keep a Silverman man, you'd better be impressive to him in some way, Zelda. Don't be lazy."

This conversation required a discussion with Grace, and so the intimacy was re-established. Zelda made the call from her bedroom with the door closed and her 'I Hear You Knocking But You Can't Come In' sign hanging from the knob. Listening to the phone ring, she pictured Grace sitting at her desk in her office at Stanford.

After Zelda filled her in, Grace said, "Dearie, you can't expect Brooke to be a mind reader. She has no idea what your standards for a relationship are."

"I don't think I know what they are, either. I fell madly in lust with Nick when I was twenty-one and married him when I was twenty-three. We now have four kids, and as you pointed out, we may not have much else in common, but four kids *are* a lot. Definitely a basis for marriage."

"Do you think you need to impress him?"

"Maybe I need to get to know what his dreams are. I want him to be happy, and I don't even know what that looks like other than the fruitful pursuit of money and trophies. He really likes money and trophies."

"Not surprising since he's surrounded by people with the same goals. But surely there's something that sets him apart from the thundering herd."

"Not really. He likes having a wife and kids, but his colossal self-esteem comes from success at work and athletic feats. His golf handicap is eight, and he hardly ever plays."

"Maybe you should spend some time with Shookie working on finding out what your idea of happiness looks like."

Zelda looked out of her window and observed the signs of approaching summer. The season was budding up, about to explode. Her tone of voice changed becoming almost philosophical. "Abraham Lincoln was a guy known to suffer from depression, and he said, 'A man is as happy as he makes up his mind to be.' Or something like that."

"I know the quote, and I think it's probably true, for the most part. And you, dearie? Is your mind made up to be happy with what is?"

"Yes. Definitely. All my kids came into this world with both hands full of love. They bring me joy every day."

"You're a good woman, Zelda. I treasure our friendship."

"I treasure it, too, and don't want it to get muddled up with Eli in anyway."

"It won't," Grace said.

"Is he coming to the book club meeting with you?"

"I expect him to. Is that a problem?"

"Not for me. He's the one avoiding me."

"Maybe that period's over." Grace's voice reflected her regret.

"Ah, the Zelda Period was very brief."

"There was no possibility of a Zelda Period. He realizes that."

Zelda's heart sank. After ending the call, she crawled into her bed and pulled the covers over her head. What would my version of happiness look like, she asked herself.

She imagined having a sparkling magic wand, which would strike Nick happy, but elsewhere—Hong Kong, perhaps—and then there she'd be, with wand still in hand, on an island in the South Pacific with Eli and her children as well as three or four of *their* children dancing on a palm-fringed beach.

Not at all what Abraham Lincoln meant, she conceded. Sitting up, she reached for pen and paper and began a gratitude list. Whenever an O'Neil kid whined or complained,

Abigail required a list be written to present to Kevin at the end of the day. Even now, these many years later, they all reverted to this method when circumstances demanded it.

Zelda dozed off while writing and woke up with the determination to appreciate things as they were.

Arriving well in advance for the book club meeting, Zelda felt eager, yet apprehensive at the prospect of seeing Eli again after nearly four months. Brooke opened the door wearing large, lightly tinted tortoise shell glasses and a black linen dress enlivened with a feathery teal scarf she'd picked up in Paris the week before.

"Great scarf," Zelda sighed.

"Eric Raisina. Rue Dauphine."

Zelda looked down to see if she was wearing the Russian bracelet. She was.

"What is this, the book club bracelet?"

"No, this is the Romanoff bracelet. I told you the story last time."

"You look just right. Intellectual, but with a house in Tahoe."

"You made my day."

Just after nine, the other women started to trickle in. Donna Hall cornered Zelda right away. "Hank says he'll come and visit us this summer."

"You know more than I do. But I'm glad to hear it."

"No one's funnier than Hank. I look forward to his calls so much."

Most of the book club members were comfortably seated by the time Grace rang the doorbell at nine-thirty. The same two young women who came to the fall meeting flanked her. But no Eli.

Brooke pecked Grace on the cheek and welcomed the PhD candidates. "Where's Eli?" Zelda could've kissed Brooke for asking.

"He'll be here in a minute. Where's the Regency atmosphere?"

"I never repeat myself."

"Wish I could say the same." Grace turned and sought out Zelda. "I hope you have some questions for me as I haven't had time to prep my group."

"Don't worry. Donna will save the day. I'll go tell her."

Before she got to Donna, the doorbell rang again, and there was Eli, tan and smiling. Donna rushed up to him, and Zelda heard her exclaim, "Eli! Elaina had such a great time last night."

Zelda strained to hear his reply, but it was drowned in ambient chatter. He was still smiling as he kissed Donna on the cheek.

Remaining rooted to her spot in the entrance hall, Zelda leaned against the arch leading to the living room. Eli made his way to her and put out his hand, not to shake hers, but to hold it. "I've missed you, Zelda."

"I've missed you, too, Eli," she breathed. She felt her heart thumping, and the air suddenly seemed thin.

By the time Zelda had caught her breath, Brooke was hustling the stragglers out of the entry into the living room to take their seats. She opened the meeting by introducing Grace and her students.

Grace asked her group to talk about their favorite Austen characters. Eli chose *Pride and Prejudice*'s Elizabeth and Darcy. He talked about the balance of reason and romance, and the compromises the characters made for each other.

In summing up, he said, "Darcy and Elizabeth are humbled by the power of love. Darcy casts his pride aside, and Elizabeth renounces her prejudice. A timeless lesson for us all."

Zelda concentrated on Eli's comments but couldn't help noticing Grace's scrutiny was on her.

At the end of the discussion, Zelda directed a question to Eli. "If Darcy hadn't been at Pemberley on that fateful day when

Elizabeth visited with her aunt and uncle, do you think destiny would have brought them together in another way?"

Eli answered almost before Zelda has stopped speaking. "I don't think they would have needed destiny. I think Darcy would have moved heaven and earth to find a way into Elizabeth's heart."

When Q and A was over, Brooke herded everyone towards the dining room. Gasps from the first to enter alerted those bringing up the rear that their hostess had done it again.

And so had Bloomers. Some of the white flowers had been partially sprayed with silver. The 'black' flowers were actually deep purple, except the pansies, which were, indeed, black and grown for the occasion. Some of them were dotted with silver paint as well.

McCall's kept to the color scheme. It was a sensation, a delicious sensation.

But Donna monopolized Eli. Once he'd departed, she came over to Zelda and said in a low voice, "I really wanted to talk to *you*, but my sister, Elaina, has a crush on Eli. So I had to scope him out."

"And what did you find?" Zelda's question sounded casual, though, of course, it wasn't, and she hated the reply.

"He's perfect for her."

Zelda bit her lip. She wanted to ask why, yet didn't want to hear Donna tell her what she already knew. She wished she could teleport herself elsewhere—anywhere deserted would do. She wanted to make primal noises, which would be inappropriate at Brooke Duncan's year-end book club meeting.

# Chapter Nineteen

Summer was almost upon them. Brooke would be in Tahoe the whole time with Taylor and Audrey, decorating the house and meeting new friends. Stuart would come only on weekends. Of course, the Blairs would be invited, but it wouldn't be the same.

Zelda had discussed summer with Shookie and decided to repeat last year's vacation. The twins were now two and the girls, six and four. Since they required such different activities, it seemed prudent to stick with a tried and true plan. And this year, the good news was that Lulu would visit her parents at the same time Zelda was visiting hers.

The trip was booked, and after announcing the details to Hank, she was genuinely astonished to discover he'd decided to devote those same two weeks to San Francisco.

"Hanky, you know Nick's going to tell me everything. Don't think I won't track your every move."

"It'll all be hearsay."

"But I'll find out anyway."

"Zelda, you're the nosiest sibling I've ever had, and if I didn't know better, I'd think you were my mother."

"Nobody thinks you're funny but you, you know."

"I didn't stalk you when you were dating Nick."

"Maybe you should've."

Zelda sulked for the rest of the day, then finally called Grace. "You're so lucky Hank's not your brother. He's *such* a sneaky guy. He found out from Mom when I'd be going east and made plans to come here."

"Don't tell me you're jealous of his spending time with Donna."

"I am. And not only that, I'm jealous of Donna spending time with him. I wanted her to be *my* friend. I know it's juvenile, but there it is."

"Fortunately, you have an appointment every week with a child psychologist."

Zelda dithered. "I don't know whether to laugh or cry. Please don't tell Eli how pathetic I am."

"Don't worry. I won't. It'd shatter his illusions."

"If he has any." Zelda's voice sounded very small. She cleared her throat and declared, "The good news is Lulu will be on Long Island while I'm there. You'd love her."

"An old friend is the world's best medicine. You'll be totally sane by the time you get back. I won't even know you."

"Are you going away?"

"Oyster Bay for a month, to stay with my brother."

"I didn't know you had a brother, much less one who's practically my neighbor."

"He lives in our parents' house. A rambling clapboard cottage right on the water."

"Can we see each other while I'm there?"

"Not sure. I didn't mention anything to you because my sister-in-law died last fall. They were married for fifty-one years, and Jeremy's been reclusive ever since."

"He must be so lonely."

"He has two sons and five grandchildren. They all live on Long Island."

"That's nice for him."

"Rose was his childhood sweetheart. I don't think either one of them ever looked at another person." Grace's voice sounded far away.

"Does he look like you?"

"He's my twin."

"Your twin! Why haven't I ever heard about this?"

"He lives three thousand miles away and hasn't been here since I met you."

Zelda's curiosity slogged on. "What did he do while you were getting your PhD and teaching English Lit?"

"He went to Wharton Business School, then worked on Wall Street until he got disenchanted. For the last twenty-five years, he's had a daily radio show on a local channel."

"What about?"

"Fishing, mainly, and other ocean-related things, like weather, pollution, et cetera."

"Fascinating. And Rose?"

"Rosie had a cooking school. Soup to Nuts, it was called."

"I don't believe it. My mother went there. My grandmother always told my mom she was the worst cook in the USA and a disgrace to the family. We're all eternally grateful for Soup to Nuts. I was about seven at the time. She and Lulu's mother went together."

"I'll tell Jeremy. He'll be so pleased."

"I've just *got* to meet Jeremy. Mrs. Weld and Lulu are the best, and you know how great Mom is. We're going to come visit you at your brother's house. Warn him."

"Hank's right about how bossy you are."

"You can *have* Hank. I'll take Jeremy."

Zelda started summer school and planned the trip to Long Island during the break. Once she got to New York, it wasn't long before she made good on her threat to descend upon Jeremy Lloyd with her mother, Lulu and Mrs. Weld. When Grace answered the door, the four women were on the porch, talking at the same time, not even pausing to notice her. She closed the door for a moment and opened it again to see all four faces looking at her in surprise.

"Come in, come in. I followed Zelda's orders and made Rosie's pink lemonade."

Introductions were made all around, and Jeremy appeared, delighted that such attractive women turned up bearing gifts prepared from Rosie's recipes. Abigail produced flourless chocolate cake, Zelda candied pecans. Georgia Weld prepared cheese straws. Lulu baked Rosie's lace cookies, which everyone agreed were the laciest.

It was droll to see Grace and Jeremy side by side, both with unruly red hair streaked with gray, thick wire-rims and compact, fit bodies. They had the same old-fashioned accent associated with that part of Long Island as well as the same zany sense of humor. They had matching facial expressions and finished each other's sentences. They could've been stand-up comics.

Abigail and Georgia recounted stories of their adventures in Rosie's school. The demonstration kitchen was about a hundred yards from the house in what was once an equipment building when the Lloyd place was a working farm, before the Second World War.

Georgia reminisced in her lazy Louisiana accent, "Jeremy, I don't know if you'll recollect this, but one fine spring day, Rosie disappeared from the kitchen, and we couldn't find her anywhere; we looked up and down and all 'round the place. Then we went out on the porch and saw you two kissin' in the herb garden. You were the cutest things!"

"Look how bashful he looks," Abigail chimes in. "I think that might have happened more than once." She helped herself to a cheese straw and continued, "Remember when that beautiful Italian woman's hair shot up in flames when she was flambéing

Bananas Foster? She was amazing. Much calmer than I'd have been, that's for sure."

Georgia added, "And the time the fryin' oil caught fire… Rosie called you, and you were there in a nanosecond with the extinguisher, like Superman or Batman to save the day, if not the lunch."

Jeremy chuckled. "She's still so alive for me. I feel her energy vibrating everywhere. Sometimes, I think if I could whip my head around fast enough, I might catch her standing behind me."

The stories and banter went back and forth until shadows had lengthened and the western sky was bursting with blazing gold. Saying goodbye was lightened by Jeremy's promise to invite Abigail and Kevin plus Georgia and Doug for dinner in the not too distant future. And he swore up and down to Zelda that he'd spend part of the coming winter in California.

Zelda called Nick every morning at eight east coast time, five a.m. in San Francisco. She wanted a full account of Hank's comings and goings on the previous day.

"Nick, I really think you should invite Donna and Hank to dinner somewhere nice. And be sure you pay strict attention to *them* and not to your *phone*. I want to know if this romance is heating up or cooling off."

"Yes, Ma'am. Anything else?"

"How are Matt and Miles?"

"We're all happy. Significant male bonding going on here."

The next morning Nick said, "As per your instructions, it's Gary Danko's tonight with Hank and Donna, Eli and Elaina. I'll keep an eye on both couples and take their temperatures every few minutes and let you know tomorrow how they're coming along."

"Why did you add Eli and Elaina?"

"I didn't. They added me."

Displeased, Zelda said, "Okay. Have fun. Kiss the twins for me. Talk to you in the morning."

The O'Neil clan had a gathering that evening, and Zelda didn't get to bed until after two. Oversleeping, she missed her chance to talk to Nick before he left for the office.

Having to wait for news of the dinner made her so cranky, Abigail said, "Zelda, if there's something bothering you, I think you should get it off your chest."

"It's nothing Mom. Just anxious to talk to Nick to see how his day went."

"You're full of surprises this morning."

Just before going to bed, she reached Nick. "How are the lovebirds?"

"Everybody's giddy with romance. I lost track of the thermometer, but I can assure you, temperatures are rising."

"Let me speak to Matt and Miles. Then I've got to get some sleep."

"You're welcome."

Zelda was tired and weepy after hearing this news. The worst part was, here she was in the same time zone as her mother, Lulu and Grace, but she had the distinct feeling that none of them would sympathize with her frustration. The next day she called Shookie, but found her out of the office and didn't leave a message.

Due to the Eli-Elaina report, Zelda was less interested in the adult news from San Francisco and made her calls later in the day, talking nonsense with the twins and schedules with Lourdes.

Zelda got Lulu included in the dreaded lunch at Marion's, and as they were Ubering over, Zelda confided, "You're making this bearable for me."

"Oh, Miss Zelda Pie, don't make a mountain out of this piddlin' little ole molehill." Lulu mimicked her mother's accent.

"You wait and see. This is quite some molehill."

"I don't think I've seen Marion since your wedding. Imagine, ten long years."

"Lucky you."

"Mom doesn't like Granny," Phoebe commented to Chloe.

"Of course, I like her. What makes you say something like that?"

Phoebe replied, "You just now said Lulu was lucky 'cause she hasn't seen her in, like, forever."

"That was only a manner of speaking."

"Whatever that means." Phoebe rolled her eyes in a comical way.

"It means Lulu is lucky to live in Jerusalem and have exciting experiences she would miss out on if she lived on Park Avenue."

"I like Park Avenue. And I like Granny and our doggie, Daisy. And Napoleon," chirped Chloe, twisting out of her seatbelt and climbing over the seat of the SUV.

Zelda re-buckled Chloe's seatbelt. "Settle down, girls. Don't rumple your dresses."

They had to ring the bell twice before Napoleon opened the door. He seemed happy, but surprised to see them. "Mrs. Blair went to the Cosmopolitan Club for a lecture-luncheon today. She didn't say you were coming."

Zelda knew relief showed on her face. "There must've been a misunderstanding. Please ask her to call and tell me when she'd like us to come back. We leave for San Francisco on Friday morning."

"But Mrs. Blair leaves tomorrow for Washington. The annual meeting she goes to. Not back until Sunday afternoon. Five o'clock."

Zelda tried not to smile. "She must have forgotten all about us."

"Not like Mrs. Blair."

"We want to see Daisy," cried the girls.

Napoleon looked uncomfortable. "Not today. I'm sorry."

"Don't worry, Napoleon. We'll go out to lunch. Give her our love." Zelda fluttered her fingers in his direction and pulled her phone out of her bag.

Before the elevator reached them, she had already pressed the Uber app and typed in the address of Serendipity. "Girls, we'll have a blast where we're going. They have magical things like frozen hot chocolate."

Lulu clapped her hands. "Serendipity! Oh, goodie! Your mother and I had a lot of fun there when we were your age. And now we're going to have some more fun with you two. Definitely frozen hot chocolate and a super long hot dog for me."

Zelda scoffed, "Lulu orders the same thing every time. It's no use sending her to live in Jerusalem and hope she'll become sophisticated enough to order grilled chicken."

"What does sophisticated mean?" Phoebe wanted to know.

"Good question," Lulu answered. "I don't think your mother knows either, if she thinks grilled chicken is sophisticated." Lulu took a compact out of her purse and put powder on her face in an exaggerated, flirty way. "Now, that's sophistication."

"It means like a movie star?" Chloe questioned.

"Not exactly, but close enough." Lulu closed her compact and tossed it back into her bag.

Phoebe thought a bit and then said, "I'll have what Lulu has."

# Chapter Twenty

*Z*elda and the girls arrived back in San Francisco late on Friday, and though Zelda was anxious to get back into General Psychology and Statistics, she was glad to hear Hank wasn't leaving until Saturday night, giving her time to scrutinize his interactions with Donna.

As luck would have it, the day had to end early for Donna. It was her grandmother's ninetieth, and the festivities started at six. While driving him to the airport, Zelda would have Hank all to herself.

With Hank safely strapped into the passenger seat, Zelda started her interrogation. "So, how's the amazing Donna?"

"Maybe too amazing to want a life with an Assistant DA."

"You want to expand on that a little?"

"Not really."

"Come on, Hanky."

"For one thing, she likes her freelance work with the *Chronicle,* and as good as she is, I don't think she could do the same thing for the *New York Times.*"

"There are other papers."

"Don't think she knows that. And have you seen her apartment?"

"No."

"It would be unattainable in New York. Multi-millions." Hank gestured vaguely, looking out the window.

"What about your moving out here?"

"She suggested that."

"Well?"

Hank didn't respond.

"You could go private." Peering at him, Zelda peered lifted her brows.

"Think Dad would disown me if I did?"

"Probably."

"Yeah. That's what I think, too." Hank opened his window.

"If she's right for you, Dad would come around. You know he would."

"I don't have to decide now. She's coming east in August. We'll see."

"Staying with you, is she?"

"Now, Zelda."

"You're never any fun." They were almost at the airport and Zelda asked as casually as possible, "So what about Elaina and Eli?"

"He's not into her." Hank yawned.

"How do you know?"

"I can just tell."

They pulled up to the Delta departure area and said a sad good-bye, making promises to talk on the phone at least once a week, promises both knew were made in vain. Easing out into the traffic, Zelda cranked up the Golden Oldies and sang along on the way home to cheer herself.

It was nearly midnight when she put her key in the latch. The hall was dark except for lazy yellow beams escaping from the lantern in the stairwell and a sliver of light coming from under the door of Nick's study.

Suddenly, Nick's muffled shouting invaded the silence of the house. Zelda froze as if guilty. She felt she was overhearing something forbidden, indecent. She crept up the stairs like a thief, ripped off her clothes and flung herself into bed. She needn't have rushed. It was hours before Nick peeled back the covers on his side.

Zelda woke first and tiptoed downstairs to the kitchen, sighing with relief when she found Lourdes already there preparing for the day.

Fifteen minutes later, Nick left for work without a word. No coffee. No, "good morning," just down the stairs and straight out the front door.

Last night's outburst replayed in Zelda's mind. One name— Don—struck her as important. From her desk in the kitchen, she phoned Brooke in Tahoe.

"Is there someone named Don at Silverman?"

"Don Peck. New-ish. Graduated from Stanford B school a year or so ago. He lives just up the street from us. Why?"

"Oh, nothing. I thought I heard Nick talking to a Don."

"Stuart says he's the most ambitious guy he's ever met. Works night and day."

"They all work night and day," Zelda said without irony.

"Just saying. Stuart thinks he's the one to watch. Want to have lunch tomorrow? I'm coming to town. I've got some great ideas for the hospital gala."

"Sure. Come here, and I'll make a salad. Bring pictures of the house. I want to see how it's coming along."

"You and Nick and all the kids are invited for Labor Day. Bring Lourdes. I've made a lot of plans."

"Sounds great."

As soon as she could, Zelda called Grace, who was still on Long Island. She blurted out, "I think we were wrong about Brooke and Nick."

After recounting the tale in a breathless rush, Zelda wanted Grace to weigh in. "So, what do you think?"

"It's possible there was no footsie at the dinner table. Ann's a romantic. And Brooke is just naturally kind of out there.

So, *I* think you're correct. We were wrong. Wonder why you haven't met this man Don, since he's on Stuart's team."

"I don't know, but I'm going to do some digging. Where's Eli?"

"In Connecticut writing his dissertation."

"Is he ever coming back here?"

"He's keeping his place in Atherton, and he'll come back for the PhD ceremony, but he's going to spend more time back East. There's a barn on his mother's property he's fixing up for himself."

"What will he do there?"

"Teach English in the public school system."

"Quite a switch from tech companies and owls."

"That was the plan after getting his doctorate."

"He's a fine man," Zelda said wistfully. "Is he still seeing Elaina Hall?"

"No idea."

Zelda went to class but was back home studying at the kitchen table when Nick burst through the garage door. She carefully marked her place and turned to him. "Brooke says Stuart thinks Don Peck is the hardest worker he's ever seen."

"Well, he's the biggest asshole *I've* ever seen." Nick opened the refrigerator door and peered in.

"What do you mean?"

"Greedy bastard who never who never lets up."

"I think that would describe most of your colleagues."

"Watch it, Zelda. You live off the fat of our profits." He slammed the door hard, making the glass bottles jangle.

"What makes this guy different?"

"Long story and none of your business." Nick's body tensed, straining to harness a powerful energy.

Sensing an attack, Zelda cringed. What was fueling him? She couldn't be sure, but stunned, she suspected it was fear.

The moment passed. Nick spun on his heel and stomped to his study, banging the door behind him.

Darkness slipped like a velvet cloak over the fog and into the house. Zelda switched on all the lights in the hall and kitchen, but it didn't dispel the miasma of foreboding.

When Brooke arrived for lunch the next day, she had a shopping bag full of samples and a phone full of photos. After discussing the décor of the Tahoe house and the plans for the long weekend, Zelda broached the subject of Don.

"So, what do you think about this guy, Don?"

"All business. No conversation."

"How old?"

"Late twenties, but already paunchy. Hideous. Zits and glasses."

"Spare me."

"He comes over all the time. On business, usually, but sometimes I think he comes just to observe Stuart. He stares intensely, head cocked to one side with drool glistening on his fat lip."

"Gross," Zelda declared.

"Maybe he'll learn something."

"Does Stuart like him?"

"Stuart likes anyone who produces." Brooke picked up her bag. "I've got to go. Thanks for lunch, and we'll talk soon about the hospital benefit. Sure you don't want to join the committee? It's going to be the best fundraiser this town has ever seen."

"Only you could do it, Brooke. I'm sure Nick will take a table."

"February twenty-seventh. Mark your calendar. You can sit with us. Tables will be expensive. Twenty grand."

"Okay, we'll sit with you and make a donation."

"I have something for the auction that's going to rock the room. A speaking part, for man or woman, on that new hospital show. It's the hottest series on TV, and the lead actor is coming to announce it. "

"How did you ever get that?" Zelda walked with Brooke towards the front door.

"Can't reveal my sources. I'm trying to finagle Stuart into buying it for me." Brooke swaggered through the hall.

"My money's on you."

"Smart bet." Brooke waved as she bounced down the slate steps, her long bare legs skimming them hurriedly. Zelda watched as her friend drove off in the navy Porsche Cayenne with a 'Keep Tahoe Blue' sticker adorning the bumper.

Feeling ashamed for indicting Brooke and prosecuting her in the courtroom of her mind, Zelda considered making amends. After all,

Brooke was just being Brooke, innocent in this and, fortunately, unaware of the accusation against her as well as the unjust verdict.

Thank God I didn't confront either of them, Zelda thought, and sank into an armchair in the living room to text Brooke: You're the best, and if you need me to do anything for the benefit, I will do it gladly, even the committee.

Brooke texted right back: It's your name I want. I want to put Zelda Fitzgerald O'Neil Blair on the invitation. Everyone will think you're related.

Zelda groaned and called Hank.

"I was wrong about Brooke having an affair with Nick. I feel terrible for suspecting them, but now, guilt has landed me on her committee."

"That's good."

"What's good?"

"That your husband's not having an affair with one of your *only* friends."

"What about the other part?"

"I do a lot of things I don't necessarily want to do for my friends, my family, my community."

"Saint Hanky." Zelda straightened a stack of garden books on the low table in front of her.

Changing the subject, Hank asked, "So, how's it going with Shookie?"

"She's on vacation, but I'll see her as soon as she gets back."

"Good. Anything else?"

Zelda could tell Hank wanted to wind it up, but she captured his full attention with her next comment. "I overheard one of those angry late-night phone calls, and I figured out who's at the other end."

"Anyone I know?"

"A guy from work. Don Peck. He lives near the Duncans. Nick was at *his* house when I assumed he was with Brooke."

"Be careful, Zelda. If things get even slightly weird, go to Grace's."

"I will, don't worry. Grace is still at her brother's in Oyster Bay, but I have keys."

As summer stretched on the Blair family got back into a smooth routine, and Zelda studied hard for the rest of the semester. She got a B and a B- in her classes, nothing brilliant, but not embarrassing either. Ready to leave her schoolwork behind, she was looking forward to going to Tahoe.

# Chapter Twenty-one

Nick took Friday of Labor Day weekend off. The whole family plus Lourdes squeezed into Zelda's Tesla and drove up to Tahoe in the morning, arriving in time for lunch.

The Duncans' house was modern, all stained wood, stone and glass, nestled in an evergreen forest, pine needles padding the curving path to the front door. Back and to the right, a small granite-lined swimming pool lay like a glittering black jewel on the woodland floor. When the Blairs arrived, Taylor and Audrey were lounging on chaises sunning themselves and called the kids to come swimming before the picnic lunch.

The striking color of the lake was always a surprise to Zelda. Today the hues of the lake, mountains and sky were almost the same, making her want to paint it, paint it in the style of Monet in his later years. These ethereal blues stirred up her gnawing hunger for beauty.

After lunch, Audrey and Taylor went with Brooke and the Blair children to the KidZone Museum, and Zelda spent the afternoon lying by the pool, gorging on the view, feeling soothed and sheltered in the arms of the pines and cleansed by the tangy balsam-scented breeze.

Towards the end of the day, her reverie was smashed by angry voices. Shouting erupted from the house. Zelda crept close.

Nick's voice was hot, but clear. "You've *got* to watch our backs."

"I don't *have* to do a goddamn thing. You and Peck got yourselves into this, Blair."

"You condoned it."

"There's no proof of that."

"Fuck you, Stuart." Crashing doors, then silence.

Zelda froze for a moment and then slunk over the pine needles back to the pool. She curled up on the chaise and covered her face with a towel, blanking her mind, listening to the breeze ruffle the air. The desire to paint had dwindled away. Her lips tightened, her breathing became shallow. A few overheard words had shifted the paradigm.

That evening the adults went to an Italian restaurant. Zelda perceived some tension between the two men, but she was certain she wouldn't have spotted it if she hadn't been alert for the signs. As the evening wore on, the conflict became more apparent, but Brooke remained focused on the social dynamics going on in the restaurant, blissfully unaware of the subtle hostilities between the men.

The rest of the weekend was serene until late Monday afternoon. While driving back to San Francisco, Zelda opened a conversation with Nick. "Did I notice some friction between you and Stuart?"

"We're together all the time. We get sick of each other."

"It seemed like more than that to me."

"Butt out, Zelda."

"Just trying to be helpful."

"*Butt out.*"

The kids and Lourdes, in the back of the Tesla, must have felt discord percolating since they remained unusually quiet during the long drive home.

Abnormal Psychology was Zelda's only course for the fall semester. Her first class was from ten until noon the day after Labor Day. She'd invited Grace for lunch, and when she returned home from campus, there was Grace, already seated at the kitchen table with the syllabus in her hands.

"I see you'll be studying 'Intimate Partner Abuse'."

All color drained from Zelda's face. "What?"

"That's what it says right here in the course description." Grace pushed the pamphlet towards Zelda, pointing to the bottom of a page.

Grabbing it, Zelda stuffed it into her bag. "I may only audit the course. It was too much this summer with all that was going on to have classes and homework."

"You have to do more than audit, if you want a degree."

"I signed up. We'll see. I'm not going to ignore my kids to get a BS."

"Of course not," Grace said. "I should go. I have a lot of paperwork to catch up on."

Hearing the sadness in Grace's voice, Zelda felt her defenses going up. "I'm sorry, but I just can't talk about it."

Grace put her arm around Zelda's shoulders. "When you're ready, dearie."

"Please don't go. Lunch is in the fridge. Just sandwiches."

"I'll have to eat and run. But why don't all of you come and have a swim on Sunday afternoon, and if Nick will man the grill, stay for hamburgers."

"It's a plan."

After seeing Grace off, Zelda went to her room and closed the door. She pulled out the course description and saw, on week seven, the class subject would be intimate partner abuse. She pulled her computer onto her lap and Googled. Half an hour later, she reached for her phone to call Grace.

"I've read up on the subject you pointed out in the syllabus and want you to know, even though some of the patterns are the same, my situation is entirely different. Mild enough to be uninteresting, really."

"So glad to hear it. I just want you and the kids to be safe and happy."

"We are. I think there's trouble at Silverman, though. Nick's under a lot of pressure, but there have been no incidents since the kitchen one. I'd say we're out of the woods, and I'm pretty sure Nick will be in town this weekend. So I'd like to take you up on that offer for Sunday afternoon."

"Would you like me to include the Duncans?"

"Not really. We've seen a lot of them lately."

"Come around four."

The afternoon at Grace's was fun for everyone, and they arrived home tired and happy at seven-thirty on Sunday evening. Lourdes met them at the door in her bathrobe.

"Mr. Duncan says to call him right away, Mr. Blair. He says it's important, no matter what time."

"Thanks, Lourdes. I'll make the call now." Nick headed for his study.

Zelda and Lourdes got the kids bathed and tucked in, and Zelda prepared for bed. Dressed in a white terry cloth robe, she was taking off her makeup when she saw Nick reflected in the mirror. She prepared herself as much as possible, curling her body forward, pressing hard into the sink.

The kicks began. Unlike prior times, it was not a single thrust. They came like stabs, over and over.

Lourdes heard the screams and appeared at the door. She slapped Nick hard in the face. "Wake up, Mr. Blair. Your wife needs to go to the hospital."

The kicking and screaming stopped. Zelda slumped to the floor, only half-conscious.

Grabbing Zelda's phone, Lourdes dialed 911. "Send an ambulance to 2499 Pierce Street!"

Nick looked down at Zelda's crumpled body and moaned. He turned away, ran down the backstairs to the kitchen and out the door leading to the garage.

Pulling a blanket and pillow from the bed, Lourdes knelt down beside Grace, covering her and cradling her head. "Mrs. Blair, can you hear me?"

Zelda nodded.

"Help is on the way. I'll check on the children and be right back."

Outside the bedroom door, the four children stood silently with their backs against the wall. Lourdes gave them a commanding look and put her index finger on her lips. She closed the bedroom door behind her and picked up Zelda's phone again, this time to call Grace.

"There has been an incident. Mrs. Blair needs you."

"I can be there in forty minutes."

"Better go straight to the hospital."

"Which hospital?"

"I'll find out and let you know."

"Can you tell me what happened?"

Hearing a siren wail, Lourdes replied, "Not now." She dashed past the children, down the stairs to open the door.

The sound of heavy boots assaulted the hushed atmosphere of the house as the four paramedics clomped up the stairs. They were wearing official-looking blue shirts and black cotton trousers. When they arrived in Zelda's bathroom, one of the men stooped down and gently asked, "Can you tell us what happened here, ma'am?"

"I slipped getting out of the bathtub."

Lourdes masked her astonishment with an expressionless face. The team moved the silent Zelda gingerly onto the stretcher.

Once Zelda was safely down all the steps and out onto the street, Lourdes said to her, "I'll stay here, and Mrs. Grace will meet you at the hospital. Don't worry. I'll take good care of the children."

Silent tears rolled down Zelda's cheeks. She reached for Lourdes' hand and squeezed it with surprising strength.

"Which hospital are you going to?" Lourdes asked the ambulance driver.

"St. Francis," he replied.

As Lourdes watched the ambulance speed away, she texted Grace the name of the hospital. On her way back upstairs, she checked and found Nick's study empty and his car gone. She quickly bolted all the doors and flew upstairs where the children were still standing in the hall, the twins holding hands and whimpering.

She hugged each of them and cooed, "Come along, my darlings. Let's make some hot chocolate." Mutely, they padded down the stairs after her.

From her car, Grace called Shookie. The call went directly to voicemail.

"I sure hope you check your messages on Sunday. Zelda's in the hospital. I don't have details, but it doesn't take any imagination to guess what happened. I'm on my way to St. Francis. The nanny is with the children, but I don't know where Nick is or what state he's in. Please help."

Despite the heavy traffic, Grace's mind raced trying to think who might know what to do with Nick. It landed on the Duncans, but something stopped her from making the call.

She pressed a button on her steering wheel and said clearly, "Call Hank O'Neil," activating the car phone again. Hank's sleepy voice answered.

"Listen, dearie. Something terrible has happened. Zelda's in the hospital. I'm on my way but have no information, and, as I'm not family, not sure how much I'll be able to find out when I get there."

"Tell me what I can do."

"Find Donna. I think she has a private number for Shookie. We need to track her down. She needs to locate Nick. I hope he won't hurt the children."

"I'm on it," Hank said and cut the connection.

# Chapter Twenty-two

Grace arrived in the emergency room just as Zelda was returning from a CT scan. While the attendants lifted her from the gurney onto the bed, Grace heard a feeble gasp and shrank from thinking how fragile her young friend looked, dwarfed by IV lines and tubes.

Taking her hand, Grace said gently, "Do you want to tell me what happened?"

Zelda shook her head. Grace could tell that even this slight movement was painful.

"You can't live with Nick anymore. Too dangerous for you and the children."

Zelda's mouth and chin quivered, but there were no tears. "Not as bad as you think."

"Zelda, for God's sake, look around. You're in the *emergency room*." Grace hardened her voice. "Nick's an adult. He knows when he chooses a behavior, it comes with consequences."

"But I don't think he wants to do this."

"He *knows*, and you've got to stop making excuses for him."

Stiffly trying to protect her ribs, Zelda's tears came but not freely. Grace found a box of Kleenex and pulled up a chair. She sat quietly by the bed until Zelda had exhausted herself.

"I won't press charges no matter what you say."

"I'm not saying you have to press charges. I'm saying you can't be alone with Nick ever again." Grace could tell Zelda

143

didn't want to listen. "I'll talk to Hank, and he'll inform your parents. No more playing with fire, Zelda."

Just then Zelda's doctor, a tall, slim man with shaggy blond hair, came into the cubicle looking grim. "We're going to need to prep you for surgery now." He turned to Grace. "I'm Pat Jackson. Are you Zelda's mother?"

Zelda answered, "This is my friend, Grace Lloyd. I have no secrets from her."

The doctor smiled at Grace, and turning back to Zelda reported, "I've looked at the films, and your spleen has been badly damaged. Ribs on both sides of your body are broken, which is contradictory to what would have happened if you'd fallen on the bathroom floor."

"I slipped and got up and slipped again," Zelda said.

"You can stick to that story as long as you want. Dr. Wong will do the surgery. He'll be here in a moment to meet you and give you consent forms to sign."

Before the words were out, Dr. Wong appeared and said, "Sorry I can't spend more time with you, Mrs. Blair, but we need to get you to the OR. Please sign these, and I'll meet you there."

The doctors turned to leave as two nurses entered with the anesthesiologist, who required a history of allergies and meds. Grace saw her chance to quiz Dr. Jackson and slipped out of the cubicle behind him.

"Dr. Jackson, wait! What's going on?"

"Her spleen has ruptured and must be removed immediately. Can you contact the family? Please assure them that she's in good hands. Dr. Wong is an excellent surgeon."

"Yes, certainly I'll contact them. Where shall I wait for her to come out of surgery?"

"We'll have a private room ready for her as soon as possible. You can stay with her here until she goes to OR."

"When she gets out of recovery, I want to be there. She shouldn't be alone."

Jackson nodded and popped his head around the curtain to talk to Zelda. "Would you like your friend to stay the night?"

"Yes. Thank you," Zelda replied weakly.

"I'll tell the hall nurse. This is not a dangerous operation, but it has to be done now. I'll be back to check on you later tonight."

Grace followed him out into the hall. "What would happen if she didn't have the surgery?"

"She'd bleed to death."

"Oh my God."

"Don't worry. We got her in time. She'll be fine, but plan on her spending a week here and at least another month of convalescence. The ribs and kidneys have to heal, too."

"That *bastard*," Grace said under her breath.

"Funny how victims want to protect those bastards." There was a weary sadness in Jackson's eyes. "I'll be back around midnight. She should be out of surgery and in her room by then."

"Thank you, Doctor."

Grace stayed with Zelda until she was rolled into the OR. By then, the room was ready, and Grace sat down to make calls. "Hank, it's bad, but she'll be okay. She's in surgery now."

Hank knew all about spleens because an associate of his was recently in a car accident, which required the same operation. He promised to break the news to their parents first thing in the morning. "Donna couldn't track Shookie down. But I talked to Lourdes. She said Nick left. I bet he's on the red-eye to New York. I bet he's running home to his mother."

"I could buy that, but I'm staying with Zelda tonight, just in case."

"I'm sure my mother will be there in time to spend tomorrow night. My father will go ballistic, of course. God only knows what he'll do."

"I'll cancel my day tomorrow and stay here until your mother arrives. And I can always stay at Zelda's and commute to Stanford. You can count on me whenever and wherever you need me. Now I have to call Lourdes before it gets any later."

"Thanks, Grace. You're a saint."

Grace called the Blair's landline, which Lourdes answered. After filling her in Grace said, "Plan on the O'Neils arriving tomorrow afternoon. I think Mr. O'Neil travels with security, so be prepared. I'll keep my cell on, and you must promise to call me if you need me for any reason at all."

"Don't worry. Everything's under control here."

"Lourdes, you're a saint."

"You, too, Mrs. Grace."

The next call was to Eli. Even though it was nearly two a.m. in Connecticut, he sounded alert and listened attentively as Grace spewed out the party line of slipping getting out of the tub. At the end of the conversation, Grace said, "Probably both parents will arrive tomorrow. I'll keep you posted by text."

"You're a saint, Gracie."

"That's what I hear, Eli."

Grace wandered down the hall to the nurse's station and asked for a toothbrush and hospital gown. She was washed and brushed and reclining in the visitors' chair when Zelda was brought in from surgery, accompanied by Dr. Jackson.

"The surgery went well," he said. "She'll probably sleep through the night. Push the call bell if she wakes up. Sleep as best you can, and I'll see you on my rounds in the morning."

Neither Grace nor Zelda moved for the next four hours and would have slept on if the nurse hadn't woken them to check Zelda's vitals. After that it was fitful sleep for another three hours, and then the clatter of breakfast woke them again.

Zelda groaned, "Ugh, I couldn't eat a thing," and pushed the tray away without looking.

Another nurse came in to examine the IV and said, "No solids for you today. But please try to get the Jell-O down."

Zelda stared at the meager offerings before her. "Do you have orange? I hate green."

"Glad you feel well enough to be fussy. I'll see what I can do."

Grace plumped Zelda's pillows and told her lies about how good her color was and how she would be up and running in no time. Dr. Jackson arrived, read the charts and reassured Grace that Zelda was in stable condition.

The nurse returned with a small paper cup of sherbet. "No orange Jell-O, but this might hit the spot."

"I can choke it down."

The neon-colored icy sweet slid down Zelda's parched throat, and soon after, she dozed off. While she slept, Grace dashed across the street and bought healthy snacks from Trader Joe's. She texted Eli that Zelda was on the mend and returned to her vigil.

Constant blood pressure readings and temperature taking annoyed Zelda, who only wanted to be left alone. Grace soothed her and worked quietly from her phone.

At four-thirty that afternoon, Grace heard a commotion in the hall, poked her head out and saw them coming. Arms linked, Abigail and a man Grace assumed was Kevin O'Neil walked towards her, flanked by four burly guards.

The five large men and Abigail continued down the wide white hall, stopping at Zelda's door. Only Abigail and Kevin came in.

"Grace, thank you for being here. Hanky told me you took charge last night. I'm forever grateful. This is Kevin." Abigail gestured towards her husband.

"How do you do, Professor? Kevin O'Neil at your service. And how's my little girl?"

Joy spread over Zelda's pinched face and tears of relief poured down. Her voice cracking, she managed, "Oh, Mom and Dad, I'm so glad you're here."

Her parents huddled around the hospital bed, stroking her hands and shoulders. Grace could almost feel their love flood Zelda's aching being, body and soul. It was like a warm balm, wrapping around her, healing and protecting her. Watching this, Grace could have sworn she'd seen energy surge into Zelda.

Kevin said, "Nick was on last night's ten-forty-five flight from SFO to JFK and is currently at his mother's apartment, but I'm not a man to take chances. Two of those guards are retired SFPD officers. They're your security detail until I say differently."

Zelda didn't have the strength to reply.

At six-thirty, Kevin checked his watch and said, "Grace, may I give you a ride? I'm going over to Zelda's before catching a plane back to New York, and I'd be happy to drop you on my way."

"My car's here, but thanks, Kevin."

"Daddy, don't go."

"I have to, Sweetheart. Mom's going to stay and so are Rudy and Frank."

"I don't need security."

Abigail piped in. "It's not for you, it's for your father. He can't sleep unless he's over-protecting you."

"Your Mom's right. I like to call anytime and get an update without waking the patient. You need to sleep and heal. When you're ready, I want you to bring those kids of yours back to New York and live with us for a while." Kevin's arm was around Zelda's shoulders. "By the way, there's a restraining order against Nick's coming within one hundred yards of you. He'll have to contact you through me."

"Yes, Daddy," she whispered and dozed off again.

# Chapter Twenty-three

A police escort, courtesy of the SFPD, sped off with Abigail and Kevin towards Zelda's house. During the short drive, Kevin called a locksmith and arranged to change not only the locks, but the codes on the garage doors as well.

Driving up the Pierce Street hill, Abigail could see the wisteria. The lavender blossoms against the red brick looked too much like the bruises she knew lay beneath Zelda's hospital gown, and she felt an overpowering sorrow.

Knowing she had to shake off this feeling for the sake of the children, she put her hand in Kevin's, gave him a kiss on the cheek and plastered a wide smile on her face. Lourdes opened the door before the O'Neils were halfway up the steps. All four children stood behind her.

Once inside the house, with her grandchildren crowding around her, Abigail's smile became genuine as she watched Kevin work his magic with the twins. Even though they could not possibly remember him, the three were soon kicking a ball around the back yard with him in the fading light.

Sitting down with the girls on the sofa in the kitchen, Abigail tried her best to answer Phoebe's questions as vaguely as possible, adroitly avoiding the issue of why Zelda was in the hospital. But she did feel confident she was telling the truth when she reassured them that their mother would be home soon and that she loved them very much.

Darkness had set in, and the children sat down for supper. Kevin paid the locksmith and stayed on to read a story and hear their prayers.

Afterwards, Kevin kissed them and slipped an envelope to Lourdes containing the new keys and five hundred dollars, saying, "Thank you for running a tight ship here, and this is for whatever you might need. My card is in there. You call me if you want anything."

He hugged his wife and was gone.

Once the children had fallen asleep, Abigail had a long hot bath and packed a canvas tote to take to the hospital.

Her phone pinged. Kevin had texted: Don't call an Uber. There's an escort outside waiting to drive you to St. Francis. Take care of our girl. I'll be back soon.

Back at the hospital, Abigail returned to Zelda's bedside and was surprised to find Grace still there. "Grace, please go home and get some rest."

"I wanted to tell you, I can easily commute to Stanford from Zelda's house, if you need me for company or carpooling the kids or anything."

"Thanks, Grace, but Lourdes has her routine with the children, and I'd never interfere." Abigail pulled a blanket over Zelda. "I'd love to have dinner with you Wednesday night, if that suits you."

"Okay, seven on Wednesday."

"I'll spend tonight here, but after that, I'll only come during the day. We have to give Rudy and Frank something to do, after all."

Zelda winced when she waved at Grace. "Thanks for everything. I don't deserve a friend like you."

"That's true, but you're stuck with me." Grace blew her a kiss.

Abigail fussed over Zelda, plumping the pillows and straightening the sheets before settling down. Then she pulled a novel out of her bag, planning on reading herself to sleep, but Brooke suddenly appeared at the door.

"What happened to you? Lourdes told me you were here."

Zelda didn't reply but looked towards her mother.

"Oh, Dr. O'Neil! I didn't see you sitting there."

Zelda preempted her mother and said, "I slipped getting out of the tub. The fall ruptured my spleen. They had to remove it."

"Oh my God, major surgery. I'll come back another time."

Abigail looked relieved. "Brooke, why don't you come on Wednesday evening? I'm going out for dinner with Grace. I'm sure Zelda would like the company while I'm gone."

"I'll do that, thanks. Feel better, Zelda. Goodnight, ladies." Not wanting to intrude further, Brooke fluttered her fingers and disappeared.

Lots of flowers were delivered the next morning. A large orchid from Kevin, a mixed bouquet from Grace, garden roses from Eli, a nosegay of violets from Donna and an extraordinary display of flowers, plants and exotic fruits came from Bloomer's with a card saying, "Love from the Duncans." Once Abigail had opened the cards and read them to Zelda, she put them in the bedside drawer and left to get some coffee.

Seeing an opportunity, Zelda asked the nurse to help her to the bathroom but not to come in. Once alone, she slowly and painfully swept the hospital gown aside and studied her torso in the mirror above the sink. Bruises bloomed around the surgical dressing over her scar, like a malignant flowers. Bright red, dark purple, greenish yellow. Horrified by the sight, Zelda limped back to bed and called Grace. "What does Eli think happened to me?"

"You slipped getting out of the tub."

"Good. Let's keep it that way."

Brooke arrived at six on Wednesday carrying a basket of cookies made by Taylor and Audrey. She hovered around Zelda but soon became bored and fidgety, finally coming right out and asking, "What time did you say you'd be going for dinner, Dr. O'Neil?"

"Why, Brooke, if you want me to leave the room, I can. I'm not expecting Grace until seven."

Brooke blushed and continued, "I didn't mean to be rude. I just thought you might've lost track of time. We usually eat earlier here than you do in New York."

"Grace has to come all the way from Stanford. But look, here she is."

"Hello, everyone. I'm early. No traffic. How's the patient?"

"Better. Let me brush my hair, and I'll be ready to go with you in five minutes." Abigail, anxious to leave, escaped to the bathroom holding her bag.

Grace stood near the bed, the last, lazy rays of the September sun glinting in her gray-streaked hair. "Dearie, you look a lot better than you did on Monday. I'm taking your mother to the Big Four on Nob Hill. Hope she'll like it."

"Perfect. She loves piano music. But watch out or she'll sit right down and join in."

"I'll keep an eye on her. Brooke, what are your plans for book club this year?"

"Contemporary fiction. Not as much fun as Jane Austen, but interesting. I was thinking, next year could be Shakespeare. Not sure if everyone would go for that, though."

"Even if they don't, I doubt anyone would have the nerve to admit it. Not to appreciate Shakespeare is really way too low-brow for your group. Anyway, it's good to stretch your mind with Elizabethan English. And all that iambic pentameter is so soothing. So zen."

"Do you ever lecture on Shakespeare?"

Grace's eyebrows shot up in mock horror. "I wouldn't dare. But I have colleagues who dare."

"It would be great, wouldn't it?"

"I think so," Grace said.

"I think so, too," Zelda chimed in.

Abigail reappeared, ready to go. "Brooke, please don't stay too long and tire Zelda. She needs her rest."

"I won't. Don't worry. Have fun."

Once the older women had left, Brooke closed the door, shutting out Rudy or Frank who was standing very close. "You know, Liane predicted I'd be visiting a friend in the hospital. But that's not the point. The point is: Where the hell is your husband?"

"I have no idea."

Brooke frowned. "What do you mean, you have no idea?" There was ice in her voice.

"We had a fight, and he wasn't home when I fell. I haven't heard from him because he doesn't know I'm here."

Brooke stopped pacing the room and turned to face Zelda. "Don't you think that's very strange?"

"I haven't even thought about it."

"I'm telling you then. It's *very* strange. He left a message for Stuart saying that he's dealing with a family emergency in New York. But who knows where he really is? He's in a shitload of trouble at Silverman. He and that Don guy are involved in some kind of money laundering."

Zelda clutched the sheet to her chest. "Money laundering?"

"In Jakarta. Those trips to Hong Kong included jaunts to Jakarta for Don and Nick. Thank God Stuart's nose is clean."

"What are you *talking* about?"

"When Don first started at Silverman, a guy from Jakarta got in touch with him, wanting to invest in a mutual fund. Only a million dollars. So Don set up a series of bank accounts to help him get the money to Hong Kong. It seems this man then wanted to add to his investment by five million US every month. Very lucrative for Silverman. But it was drug money."

"I can't believe Nick would do anything like that." Zelda smoothed her hair with a shaking hand.

"He didn't know at first, but even after they knew, he and Don kept on doing it. They're in real trouble. Maybe even jail time if word gets outside the company."

"How could Stuart not have known?" Zelda remembered the conversation she'd overheard in Tahoe.

"Stuart was as surprised as we are. He had no idea."

"This seems unbelievable to me." Zelda moved, uncomfortably pulling her hospital gown tight around her. "When did you find out?"

"Monday night. I came straight here."

"Brooke, listen, I don't have my phone here. Nick's probably been calling. We had a fight, and he left the house. I haven't had time to wonder what happened."

"I find this very weird." Brooke looked worried and started pacing again. "He's your husband, and you don't even know if he's in New York?"

"Brooke," Zelda said in a small voice, "We had a fight, he left. I'm mad at him. I don't want to think about him."

"But the kids. You think he's with the kids?"

"Lourdes is with the kids. I didn't ask Nick where he was going when he left. Then I slipped and came here in an ambulance."

"I'm sorry, Zelda. I don't want to upset you, but you need to find out what's going on. Maybe your mother didn't say anything about Nick not being home because she thought you knew that he was on a business trip or something. Let me tell you this, wherever he is, he is *not* on a business trip. He's *hiding* from an in-house investigation."

"I'm too tired to talk about it tonight. I'll tell Mom in the morning. She can find out. Or Dad can. Thanks for the flowers and fruit and thank the girls for the cookies."

"I can tell you're exhausted. But deal with this first thing, and let me know where Nick is. Stuart *needs* to know."

As soon as she thought Brooke was safely out of earshot, Zelda took her phone out of the bedside drawer and called her father. She related the entire exchange with Brooke and the conversation she'd eavesdropped on in Tahoe. She also brought up Nick's shouted exchange with Don.

Kevin was silent during her recitation. "I knew most of this, and I assumed Stuart was in on it. I don't really care what happens to any of these guys as long as you and the kids are safe, but whether I like it or not, Nick is the father of my grandchildren, and I'll do what I can to mitigate what happens to him. This is not in my sphere of influence, but I know some people."

"You know some people, Dad? You sound like a gangster on TV."

"I should be so lucky."

"What can I say to Brooke tomorrow?"

"You tell her you spoke to me. Tell her I confirmed Nick is in New York, staying at his mother's apartment. He needs to cooperate with the investigation."

"I know."

"Tell Brooke I told you not to discuss this with anyone. And tell her I'm getting you legal representation. That ought to get her off your back."

"Yes, Daddy."

"You rest and heal and let me handle this."

# Chapter Twenty-four

On Friday morning the sun streamed through Zelda's fourth floor window, waking her and filling her with hope. When she opened her eyes, the first things she saw were her mother, sitting close by and the doctor, standing at the foot of her bed reviewing her chart.

"How about letting me go home today?"

"I can't let you go, yet. There's still blood in your urine from the damage to your kidneys. Otherwise, you're healing nicely. Dr. Wong did a great job."

"What about Monday? Can I leave on Monday?" Zelda asked.

"If your urine is clear, you can go, but no lifting anything for a couple of months. Those ribs will take some time to heal."

"Whatever you say, Doctor."

"Don't forget, you need to see Dr. Wong for a six-week checkup before you go making any plans. You have to take it easy."

Happy to hear that Zelda's hospital stay was coming to an end, Abigail said, "Thanks for everything, Doctor," and phoned her husband to give him the news. "Frank and Rudy have been so nice, but we really don't need security."

"They stay put until I get there. I'm arriving next Friday, then flying back with you on Sunday."

"Grace will stay at Zelda's after we leave. Then, as soon as Zelda's strong enough to travel, she'll come to us with the children."

"By that time, we'll know what's going on with Nick." Kevin's voice sounded grim.

Monday afternoon, Zelda got the okay to go home. Even though her mother was there, attending to every detail, Zelda felt drained. The optimism of Friday morning had clouded over like the sky, which was now almost black. Anxious to see her children yet dreading having to answer their questions, she left St. Francis after the eight-day stay with mixed feelings.

Her children had made brightly colored collages and drawings to welcome her home, and accepting the explanation they'd been given didn't question her at all. Slipping getting out of the bath seemed natural to them, and Daddy away on a business trip was normal. In Zelda's bedroom there was a small bouquet of palest pink roses with a card signed by her mother.

Abigail directed operations and allowed the children to play quietly in Zelda's room but only on the floor. No bouncing on the bed! She explained about the ribs, and they treated their mother with care.

By the time Kevin O'Neil arrived on Friday night, Zelda was feeling strong enough to go downstairs. Although she didn't feel up to getting dressed, she brushed her hair and rubbed bronzer on her pale cheeks, greeting him in the living room wearing her terry cloth robe. Sensing his distress, she steeled herself for what was to come.

Kevin hugged Zelda cautiously and helped her into an armchair next to the sofa. Zelda seemed so slight and fragile that Kevin's breath caught in his chest. He cleared his throat.

"The most important thing is you and the children will be alright. But I have some bad news. Nick's financial situation is precarious, and this house is heavily mortgaged. The overhead here is very high, and Nick juggled your lifestyle paycheck-to-paycheck, spending his bonuses before they came in.

"He has nothing saved, not a penny to his name."

Zelda looked around her well-appointed living room in dismay. Everything had been chosen by the decorator, but she liked the cheerful colors and the soft comfort of the furniture and lighting. Nick had never told her to cut back on anything. The lacquered apricot paint job in this room alone had cost almost a quarter of Hank's yearly salary, and the heavy silk curtains on all four windows, pooling on the floor, well, she shuddered to think. Nick had insisted that Zelda use Brooke's interior designer and never batted an eye at the expense.

"What about the Silverman stock?" Zelda asked.

"He has some, but it's not liquid. Not sure how that works, but it's not enough to affect your situation."

Choking back the gasp that unsettled her ribs, Zelda winced. "What's going to happen?"

"I don't know. But you and the kids can come live with us when you're strong enough to travel."

Zelda turned to her mother. "Did you know about this, Mom?"

"Your father told me last night."

Shocked, Zelda shifted uneasily in the down-filled chair. She wrapped her arms around her middle and rocked cautiously backwards and forwards, saying nothing for a few moments.

Kevin and Abigail stood still, waiting for their daughter's response.

Looking up at them, Zelda finally spoke. "None of this ever mattered to me. It was just a stage-set for the life Nick wanted us to live. I never got into it." She took a few shallow breaths. "My children are healthy. Right now, that's all that matters."

The O'Neils visibly unwound and relaxed onto the sofa. Kevin said, "I talked to Dr. Jackson today, and he told me you're coming along fine. I think we can count on your being with us by late October."

"I'll throw a Halloween party with all the cousins at our house and arrange for kindergarten and play groups. You don't have to worry about any of that." Abigail was in her element.

"You're the master of family-life structure, Mom."

"Your mother is going home with me on Sunday. She has some things she wants to do in preparation for your arrival. Grace says she'll be here before we leave. You're lucky to have such a good friend."

"I know. And the best news is, when she retires, she's going to move in with her brother in Oyster Bay."

"Everything will work out as it should." Abigail reached for her husband's hand.

"What about Lourdes? Can we afford to keep Lourdes?"

Kevin glanced at Abigail, squeezed her hand and replied, "For the moment, yes. We'll have to see how things go, but let's say we'll reassess the situation in March. That gives us six months."

"Coming back home will be an adjustment for you." Abigail looked at her daughter with compassion and thought how thin and pale she'd become.

"Not really. I know the ropes. The kids will be with me. We'll be fine."

"You're a good sport, Zelda." Kevin got up and patted her on the back. "I'm going to leave you ladies. I've got a report to read. See you in the morning."

It was already nearly ten, but Abigail and Zelda stayed in the living room, finding comfort in each other's company and discussing the logistics of the move from San Francisco. Zelda sipped some ginger tea and Abigail had a glass of white wine.

They made a plan to put the house on the market in December. Zelda didn't want any of the furniture, so selling it furnished seemed sensible. Nick could take whatever he wanted out of the house after she and the children moved to New York.

"Let's hope Nick goes along with this. He could object, you know," Abigail said.

"I wonder where he'll live. Neither one of us has roots here. He may go back East, too."

"Your father is looking into what arrangements can be made for the children. He wants to find a Mary Poppins-type security agent to accompany them on their visits to Nick. What do you think the chances are of finding her?"

"Somewhere around zero to two percent, I imagine. And I really don't think Nick would ever harm them."

Shooting her daughter a stern look, Abigail put her hand on Zelda's arm. "You can't be too careful. And, believe me, your father would never allow them to go alone. Even if it was just to Marion's Park Avenue apartment."

"I know, and I'm so glad the decision is out of my hands. He's right, really."

"Tomorrow you should walk around the house. I'm sure there are some things you'll want."

Looking around blankly, Zelda said, "No, Mom, I don't want anything except the photographs and maybe some linens. I like everything, but it's more Nick than me. I don't know what my taste is, but it's not this."

"I'm sure Nick will be glad to hear that."

"I don't have any animosity towards him."

"Well, you *should*, Zelda. He put you in the hospital and wrecked your marriage permanently." Abigail took her hands. "Please go talk to Shookie. It's not natural not to feel angry."

"You're right. But all I feel is empty."

"Maybe she can help you with this."

"I don't want to feel anything."

Hearing this almost broke Abigail's heart. "Go see her and tell her."

Zelda sighed. She knew when she was defeated. "Okay, if you insist."

"I insist, and I'm going to ask Grace to make sure you make an appointment this week."

It was after midnight when the women went upstairs to bed. While brushing her teeth, Zelda thought not having direct contact with Nick would seem strange but admitted to herself that it was a great relief, too. What could she ever say about that Sunday night? Finally hitting the sheets, she dozed off quickly. But in the guest room, Abigail tossed and turned. Dawn's golden tentacles were caressing the night by the time she drifted off.

Before Zelda knew it, the weekend was over and her parents had gone. Grace, now installed in the pink guest room, started talking while Zelda helped her unpack. "Look, dearie, I promised your mother I would get you to Shookie. I made the appointment and will take you there in the morning. I'm having a hair emergency so I'll leave you with her and come back after I've tended to my hair."

"A *hair* emergency?"

"I've decided to get rid of the gray. Now that I've decided, I want to do it before I change my mind."

"This is big news. What color are you going for?"

"Restoration to its natural, brilliant red. God only knows what that'll cost and how much time it'll take. But I booked you for a double with Shookie, so you probably won't have to wait long for me."

"You won't look like Jeremy anymore. No one will believe you're twins ever again."

"That's right. I'll look like his very much younger sister, and I'll delight in gloating over that satisfactory turn of events. I don't know why I didn't do this years ago."

"What brought this on now?"

"Yesterday, I was in a mirrored hall with some other professors. While we were chatting, I caught sight of an old woman standing with some young women, and I thought who *is* that? She looks very old, but *very* familiar. I waved at her, and she waved back. In fact, I was she. Terrible shock."

Zelda laughed and shook her head. "You always look good to me, Gracie."

"If you take good manners too far, Zelda, it becomes hypocrisy. You're now officially on the verge."

# Chapter Twenty-five

A t twelve-thirty Grace strode through the door into Shookie's neon-hued, child-centric waiting room. Zelda was startled to see her friend looking so much younger.

"Oh my God, I love your hair!"

Grace beamed with pleasure, and they chatted animatedly on the drive to Balboa Café on Fillmore Street. People-watching and delicious food were sure to cheer Zelda, Grace thought, so she'd chosen this wood-paneled pub-like bistro for lunch.

Although Zelda's hair was darker than Grace's—auburn, rather than red—they now looked somewhat alike, and while pouring water, the waiter at the Café said, "I know sisters when I see them."

After placing the order, Grace remarked, "If I didn't have to wear these glasses, I'd go get false eyelashes, too."

"Stop, Grace. Now you're the one officially on the verge. I don't know on the verge of what except, possibly, lunacy. Please don't tell me you'd wear false eyelashes."

"I'm glad you didn't add, 'at your age'."

"They just don't go with Jane Austen."

Grace sipped her water. "Maybe they should, on some occasions."

"But not all the time."

"As you see, I didn't do it."

"I think you might, though."

"You never know with people like me." Grace batted her meager lashes and rolled her eyes.

"You look very glamorous as is."

Zelda's Cobb salad and Grace's eggs Benedict arrived. Zelda exclaimed over the presentation of her salad as Grace dug in. They ate in happy silence, then Grace broke it saying, "I feel new. So glad I invested in this chemical enhancement. I may look into others."

"Brooke should be your consultant. She knows every single thing concerning youth and beauty. She used to sell Sisley at Saks' in Palm Beach."

"Let's invite her over this week. I'm suddenly fascinated."

Zelda's eyes widened. "Have you met someone you're not telling me about?"

"No one. Just my reflection in the mirror. I don't think I've known what I look like in a very long while."

"I'm going to call Brooke right now."

Zelda fished in her bag for her phone. Looking around and seeing enough space between tables, she put it on speaker. Brooke answered right away.

"Grace is interested in a makeover, and you're just the advisor the professor needs."

"I've always wanted to get my hands on her. She's got great bones."

"How soon can you come?"

"How about this afternoon?"

Grace shook her head. "I have something I have to do at three but could be back before seven."

Brooke said, "Zelda, ask Lourdes to fix some sandwiches, and I'll bring a bunch of stuff over. Stuart is out of town, so we have all night to experiment. I'll get there early. There are a few things I want to discuss with you."

Grace dropped Zelda home after lunch with strict instructions to have a nap. Wondering why Brooke wanted to come early made Zelda apprehensive, impeding her sleep.

Zelda was lounging on a sofa in the living room when Brooke arrived. Twilight had crept into the house, and Brooke punched the master light switch after she burst through the door, a whirlwind of autumn-colored cashmere. As it turned out, Brooke was mainly interested in the dance she was planning for the hospital benefit and didn't quiz Zelda about Nick. She stood in front of Zelda and recited the detailed plans she'd made for invitations, decorations, flowers, menu and venue.

Then, almost as an afterthought, she said, "Stuart said Don is staying in San Francisco, and Nick is being transferred to New York. Good thing Silverman doesn't shoot their wounded. Nick still has a job, and I expect you to come back for the gala."

Zelda's abdomen had tightened at the mention of Nick's name, and the very thought of his living in New York drained her face of all color.

"Sit down Brooke. There's something I have to tell you." Once Brooke was settled in the armchair next to the sofa, Zelda swung her feet to the floor and sat up straight. "Nick and I are separated, and I'm taking the children to live at my parents' for a while. I wanted to wait before telling anyone, but obviously you know more about Nick's career than I do. I didn't even know he was being transferred."

The corners of Brooke's mouth turned down. "Liane saw this in my chart. She said someone close to me was going to leave me in the lurch."

"But, Brooke, this isn't about you."

"It *is* because I was expecting you to help me with the ball. Anyway, I'm keeping your name on the invite. When are you leaving?"

"End of next month."

"You can come back in February for the party."

"I can't make any promises. And I thought you didn't need any help."

"Moral support. I count on you for that."

"I can give you that from New York."

"Oh, please. Not the same, and you know it."

At this point, Grace arrived wearing a suede jacket, brief-case in hand. Taking one look at Zelda, she said, "Let's get you into bed. We'll bring a tray."

Brooke jumped up and grabbed Grace by the shoulders. "Oh, my God, the color's epic. I can't wait to finish the job."

"I insist on watching the makeover." Zelda stood carefully, holding onto the arm of the sofa.

"We'll do it in your room but with you tucked in."

After supper, Brooke took charge, and with powders and pencils, she transformed Grace. Zelda clapped her hands. "Grace, you certainly can't think your reflection looks old now."

Grace smiled sheepishly, and Brooke said, "Nothing's free, Grace. I want you to buy an emerald green evening dress, get contact lenses, and come to my hospital gala on February twenty-seventh. You'll be my guest and so will your escort."

"My brother will be in town then. Not sure he still has a tuxedo, but I'll inquire."

"I'm counting on you to bring up the level of conversation at the table. I hear from Zelda that your twin is a radio host. That's perfect as we have another entertainment industry person at the table as well. Ethan Wilder from the TV series *Healing Arts*. He's big. *Really* big."

"Well, Jeremy is small, *really* small. I hope Ethan won't be disappointed."

"Ethan will be seated between you and me so he *definitely* won't be disappointed."

"What on earth will I talk to him about?"

"You're a Stanford professor. It doesn't matter what you say." Brooke still had the blush in her hand and swept Grace's cheek one more time. "He'll be impressed. And he'll have *me* on the other side."

"And who will I have on my other side?"

"I don't even know who's coming yet. And Stuart likes to think he seats the table, but probably your brother. You can keep all this makeup. For the ball, I'll have my daughter, Taylor, do your face. She's as good as anyone I've ever seen with lashes. You'll love it."

Grace looked over at Zelda. "See, there *are* occasions for professors to wear false eyelashes."

"Brooke, you've made this professor's dreams come true. I'll try my best to come back for the party."

"And I'll tune into *Healing Arts* a few times so I'll know what Ethan looks like in case I can't see through contacts and lashes," Grace said.

The following evening, Grace returned from work with some news. She found Zelda in the kitchen setting the table for supper. "Eli has some business here and is coming out next week for a few days. He doesn't know you and Nick are separated and asked if we could all go out for dinner."

Zelda felt her pulse quicken and finished her task before replying. "Tell him Nick will be out of town, but I would love to go."

"Will you feel up to going out?"

"Not sure. Maybe we should eat here."

"As long as it doesn't stress you. I could get take-out."

"Lourdes has a cousin who's a good cook. She was here all day filling up the freezer with soups and casseroles. We're having her chicken potpie with the kids tonight. Much better than take-out."

That night, after the children were in bed, Zelda and Grace tuned into *Healing Arts* on the huge flat screen in the guest room, each of them stretched out on a twin bed. They loved it and agreed that Brooke was a genius with parties. Having a part on the show to auction off and landing this hottie to announce it would make the evening news in San Francisco.

As the day of Eli's arrival got closer, Zelda began to perk up. She looked at the labels on the containers in the freezer and decided on chili. Lourdes would prepare the garnishes, and her cousin would make her famous key lime pie.

The morning of the chili dinner, Grace came to Zelda's room to find her already up, towel-drying her hair.

"Look, dearie, I think I have to tell Eli you're separated. If he found out from anyone else it would be strange."

"Okay," Zelda said uneasily and gave Grace a stern look. "But stick to the 'slipping-while-getting-out-of-the-bath' story."

"Of course." Grace stepped backwards, avoiding drops of water flying from Zelda's hair.

"You might disapprove of lying, but I want to keep this secret for the children's sake."

"I respect your privacy. What does Shookie say?"

"She wants me to be aware of the reality of the situation. But she says it's up to me if I want to tell anyone."

"Agreed." Grace said 'good-bye' and left for Stanford.

That evening, with Grace standing next to her, Zelda felt comfortable seeing Eli again. He complimented Grace on her new look, and by the time the chili was on the big oak kitchen table, everyone was at ease. Eli had a way with kids and had them laughing in no time. He stayed after dinner and even joined in on bedtime reading. But when it was time to say goodnight to Zelda, Eli looked awkward.

She saw him to the door. He stood on the top step and said, "Great to see you recuperating so well. If you feel up to it, I'd like to take you and Grace out before I go back East."

"How long are you here?"

"My flight leaves the day after tomorrow, but if tomorrow night doesn't work for you, I could change it."

"Tomorrow is fine."

"I'll pick you up at seven." He turned reluctantly and walked slowly down to the street. Zelda watched him, and as he reached his car, he looked back. She saw his silhouette outlined by the lanterns flanking the bottom steps. He touched his fingers to his lips and, with a flick of his wrist, sent the kiss to her.

# Chapter Twenty-six

The next day, Zelda lolled around the house and thought about what to wear for dinner with Eli. When Grace came home, late in the afternoon, she went straight to Zelda's cream-colored bedroom. "I have a splitting headache, dearie. Can't possibly go out with you kids tonight."

"Maybe I should cancel." Zelda held her breath, willing Grace to disagree.

"Why would you do something like that?"

"People don't know I'm separated."

"Well, Brooke knows, so Stuart knows. And, of course, Shookie knows, and I bet Hank told Donna. Who cares, anyway?"

Zelda tilted her head, considering. "You're right."

"As usual." Grace turned and marched out towards the guest room.

Eli sounded insincere saying he was disappointed that Grace was not coming and drove off with Zelda in high spirits. Over dinner at a casual neighborhood restaurant, Zelda told him she was moving back in with her parents. This sparked an animated conversation about the public school system in Connecticut as opposed to New York.

"I'm looking forward to my children going to school with their cousins at the same Catholic school I attended."

Saying goodnight proved to be tricky. Neither of them wanted to end the evening, neither could bear to make the first move. They sat in Eli's Jeep outside Zelda's house for nearly half an hour without touching or having any sort of meaningful exchange. Finally, Eli got out and opened Zelda's door. Holding her elbow, he piloted her up the steps.

Zelda murmured, "I can't believe I won't be here to see the wisteria bloom again."

Eli sprang to life. "We have *plenty* of wisteria at Blendon Farm! It climbs up and around a pergola making an awning over the porch. You'll come and visit me there."

"And you'll come to the city and meet your New York colleagues."

This cheered them up sufficiently to say goodbye with dry pecks on each other's cheeks.

Grace's headache must have disappeared as she was in the kitchen boiling water for tea when Zelda arrived. There was a jumbo package of Oreos open on the counter. "Tell me how you found Eli."

"He loves teaching and likes living in Connecticut. He doesn't even seem to dread the impending winter."

"Do you?" Grace helped herself to several Oreos.

"Not a bit. I've missed it, like an old friend."

"I don't miss it at all. If I need to say 'hello' to snow, I can go to Squaw Valley. A veritable winter wonderland rather than dirty, old snow piled up along the roads."

Zelda leaned her elbows on the counter. "Have you ever been to Blendon Farm?"

Grace nodded and poured the hot water over a bag of China tea. "Lovely. It's on the Connecticut River. The house was built in 1880, and Beatrix Farrand designed the garden in the 1920s. Ann has impeccable taste. Everything is exactly as it should be."

"I've been invited there when the wisteria is in bloom." Zelda's voice was soft and wistful.

"Heaven." Grace sipped her tea. "Dining on that porch in June with a full cricket orchestra in the background. Really, heaven for all the senses. I can almost conjure up the fragrance now."

"Did Eli grow up there?"

"He's a New York City kid."

Zelda looked up, surprised. "He never mentioned that."

"He's lived here since he was an undergraduate at Stanford. But his parents didn't buy Blendon until about fifteen years ago, when they retired. Eli's father, Clifford, was a character. An old-fashioned newspaperman and editor of the *New York Post*."

"I wonder if he knew my family or Nick's."

"Doubt it. Cliff and Ann both worked very hard, and all of their friends were either journalists or doctors. With the exception of Jeremy and Rose. We all met in Florida when Eli was twelve. I told you that."

"But you didn't mention Jeremy."

"You didn't know him then." Grace carried her cup to the sink.

"When did Eli's father die?"

"Two years ago. Emphysema. Three packs a day. Last of the big-time smokers."

Zelda grabbed an Oreo before Grace stashed the rest of the package in the cupboard.

"Ann and Jeremy are still best of friends. He would have joined us in Antarctica for Christmas if his kids hadn't pitched fits. After Cliff died, Rose and Ann were inseparable. Now with Rose gone…"

"It's nice your families are close. My family is so big, we don't have room for others."

"What about the Welds?"

"You're right. We've got a lot of family friends in the neighborhood, really. I'm looking forward to going back there to live. Such good people."

"I'm glad you're happy about that. You've been through a lot lately." Grace moved around the kitchen, putting things to right.

"Sometimes I feel like I'm holding on by a thread, but I know how to suck it up. My father trained us well." Zelda straightened her spine as if her father were right there inspecting her posture.

"You'll get stronger every day."

"Thank God for the kids."

Grace gave the counter a final wipe. "It's going to be alright, but your mother's spot on about seeing Shookie as often as you can."

"I've got another appointment tomorrow. I'm working through this in my own way."

Grace lifted her brows dramatically.

"*What*?" Zelda sounded offended. "I *am*, really, I am."

The month raced by, and the last week was frantic. Zelda barely managed a final look around the house. On a coffee table in the living room, she spotted a specimen marble box she'd bought in Florence. She picked it up and held it to the light, remembering the day she found it had been filled with firsts for her.

She thought of the Ponte Vecchio, the *duomo*, the David and made a decision to keep a piece of that sunny morning in March with her wherever she went. She ran to the kitchen and grabbed a dishtowel, wrapped the small box up and dropped it into her carry-on.

It was cold and rainy when they arrived at Kennedy airport early the next morning. Her mother and Mrs. Weld were there to greet them, both driving large SUVs. Even so, there was hardly enough room for four adults, four children, car seats and all the luggage.

The following week was filled to overflowing with family, friends and Halloween, but by early November, Zelda was on the phone every day to Grace. Although she didn't acknowledge her longing to hear about Eli, repressing any awareness of it, she hoped every time they spoke Grace would talk about him. This never happened, and one rainy afternoon in early December, she went to her room and called Grace, determined to bring him up.

"Grace, when are you coming East?"

"I arrive on the twenty-second and spend two nights with Jeremy then drive up to Connecticut on the twenty-fourth to spend five days with Ann and Eli."

Zelda inhaled sharply but hoped Grace couldn't hear it. "Sounds good," she mumbled.

"How about spending New Year's Eve with Jeremy and me? Plan to stay the night. Night driving in winter is hazardous at best, and New Year's Eve just makes it worse. Bring those candied pecans you made last summer, and invite anyone you want to come as well."

"Everyone in my family has their usual New Year's Eve plan. They've all sweetly told me I'm welcome to join in, but I'd much rather have a plan of my own. Coming to you would be perfect. I can get there early and help you cook."

"Then come on the day before, the thirtieth."

"Great!" Thrilled with this news but wanting to take the spotlight off it, she changed the subject. "What are you doing for Thanksgiving?"

"I'm going to Rupert and Kirk's. Remember them? Math and physics?"

Turning down the covers on her bed with one hand, Zelda climbed in. "Give them my best regards."

"Very formal, Zelda."

"I *am* very formal these days."

"Now tell me how you really are." The worry in Grace's voice was apparent.

"My marriage will be dissolved by the State of New York sometime next year. Nick is living at his mother's and working at Silverman Midtown. My lawyer tells me Nick's responsibilities and salary have been reduced, but he's hanging in there. The kids haven't seen him yet. An agreement has to be worked out first."

"Not easy."

Nervous energy crackled through Zelda. She got out of bed and straightened the photographs littering her dresser. "Dad is insisting on armed security for the visits, and there's no objection from Nick, so I guess he'll see them soon. But I'm not going. I can't."

"Of course not."

"Thanks for always understanding."

"Are you having telephone appointments with Shookie?"

"Twice a week." Zelda nodded. "Phoebe seems to be cured, whatever that means. No more interest in talking to Shookie and no acting out."

"That's good."

"Yep. And Mom runs a great household. We're all happy here. I need a job, though. Getting low on funds. I have an interview at Sanctuary for Families. I'll volunteer at first. Have to get certified for paid employment."

"That would be a healing place for you to work, but what about finishing your degree?"

"I'll have to do that at night. I'll get half of whatever the house sells for after the mortgages are paid off, but that won't be much."

"At least it's something."

"It'll give me babysitting money for dozens of my nieces and nephews."

"Where's Lourdes?"

"She's still here, but she wants to go back to the Dominican Republic. Her sister called last night, and apparently, her childhood sweetheart is back on the market. She needs to get down there and check him out."

"Lucky Lourdes. Childhood sweethearts are the best."

# Chapter Twenty-seven

December thirtieth was a busy day for Zelda, and she didn't arrive in Oyster Bay until late afternoon. Jeremy's house looked festive, sparkling in the snowy landscape with multicolored lights. When she reached the top of the winding driveway, she could see through a front window that his Christmas tree was still up. Heaving her suitcase out of the back of her mother's SUV, she stopped to gaze westward. The sky was ablaze, flaunting intense tangerine and pink visions low on the horizon, capped by banks of deep purple clouds. The beauty touched off a surge of hope in her heart, and she raced up the steps to ring the doorbell with joy.

"Dearie," Grace said, swinging the door wide, "you're just in time. Get in here and help. Anything other than Beef Stroganoff and tuna casserole is beyond my capabilities. Jeremy thought he made it easy for me asking me 'just' to do the vegetables and dessert for tomorrow night."

Grace swept Zelda into the house and took her coat while steering her towards the stairs. The entrance hall was lined with marine watercolors, which wandered up the stairway and crept into the upstairs hall. Zelda had admired them last summer but had not taken in the whole collection. She stopped mid-way up to look at a lighthouse painted against an evening sky. This was a picture of the hope she felt. Somehow, she thought, she would be guided through this confusing time.

"Come on. No time for art appreciation now. We've got work to do."

"How many are we tomorrow night?" Zelda followed Grace up to the guest room.

"Tonight, it's just you and me. Ten tomorrow. Beef Wellington with crab cakes to start. Jeremy did his part, and then departed. He's playing poker tonight." Grace opened the bedroom door.

Happy with the knowledge of having Grace to herself for one night, Zelda flung her suitcase on the bed. "Who's coming tomorrow night? Anyone I know?"

"You know everyone except my old friend Eliza Achilles. She's the dean of a girls' school in Virginia. A spinster, like me, and very amusing."

"Also like you."

"Okay, what are we going to feed everyone for veg and dessert?" Grace asked, adjusting her glasses.

"Sounds substantial already, so what about cauliflower purée and peas?"

"Then what? I hope to spend as little time as possible in the kitchen."

Zelda tossed her things in a drawer and looked around the room. It reminded her of an inn where she'd once stayed in Maine. A colorful oval rag rug covered most of the floor and starched ruffled organdy curtains hung at the windows. The bed had a maple headboard and a white chenille bedspread.

She turned to Grace. "I remember your Neapolitan ice cream slices were a big hit."

"Don't know where to find them here."

"What about Klondike Bars? We can throw the wrappers far away and serve them with berries and whipped cream. Everyone will think it's Tartufo."

"Good idea. Let's go to the grocery store now and then out to dinner."

They made a list and trudged out into the icy darkness, snow crunching beneath their boots as they cut across the frozen lawn to Grace's car. A west wind had blown away the clouds. The sky was dazzling, spangled with brilliant stars, the sharp air fragrant with wood smoke.

After shopping, returning home and getting the groceries put away, they went to Wild Honey and ordered burgers. Grace handed the menus back to the waiter and said to Zelda, "Tell me how the children like their first New York winter."

"They love it. Snow is magical stuff, and my whole family is dedicated to making us feel at home."

"And Nick? What's going on with him?"

"The kids went with their pistol-packing Mary Poppins to meet him at Marion's on the twenty-fourth for lunch. It was the first time they'd seen him since that night."

Grace made a circular gesture for more information.

"Kids are resilient. They came back with their presents and a tale about Daisy, the dog, having moved to a farm upstate. Poor old Daisy. They liked Mary Poppins but didn't say much about Nick or Marion. Shookie said not to quiz them, so we didn't."

"You mean to tell me they don't mope around all day and ask a lot of difficult questions?"

"They have twenty-two first cousins. Remember, I'm the youngest of eight. They're having the time of their lives."

"What about Lourdes?"

"She's in the D. R. checking out that sweetheart. I don't think she'll be coming back. We miss her, but all my brothers and sisters live in the neighborhood, so there's no lack of sitters. Lourdes promised to come back and visit us, and I'll go down for the wedding, if she decides to marry."

The waitress arrived with the burgers, ketchup and mustard. "Who gets rare?" Grace raised her hand.

"Who babysits?" Grace shook the ketchup bottle with all her might.

"I have a niece majoring in business admin. She's taken charge of the schedule. She says it's like running a small company. I pay them ten percent above the going rate for their age groups. Two on duty at a time. So far, so good."

Grace held her burger in both hands, elbows on the table. "What happens when your sitters are at school?"

"It hasn't been a problem so far, and there's a possibility of an au pair from Ireland. Mom's looking into it."

"Does Hank tell you anything about Donna?"

"Hank? Oh, that Hank! He keeps his cards very close to his chest, but when Donna was here in August, she met the entire crew. Hank is my only unmarried sibling, so as you can imagine, the status of their relationship is a hot topic. He's out there for New Year's." Zelda dragged a French fry through ketchup.

"That's a big deal."

"I'd say so. My sister, Dot—that would be Dorothy Parker O'Neil Sanchez—has a party planning business. She also happens to be the bossiest in the family, except, maybe, Dad. Anyway, she's planning on planning everything for the potential couple. Don't think that'll sit well with Donna."

"Or her mother."

"Dot's very persuasive, though, and very talented, too. We'll see. By the way, I've been watching Brooke's auction item on TV."

"Really? And what do you think of *The Healing Arts*?"

"I'm hooked."

"Me, too."

After dinner, they lingered in the candlelight until it became apparent that others were waiting for the table. Grace paid the check, and they walked into the cold night. A few snowflakes drifted down, but the stars were still bright, no sign of a storm.

Jeremy wasn't back from his poker game when they got home, so Grace lit a fire in the library and took a deep breath. "Now, I want to know about your own healing, Zelda."

Zelda settled back into an armchair and crossed her legs. "I've started the volunteer work I told you about."

"That sounds challenging," Grace said.

"It's empowering for me to use my experience to help others. I had it so easy compared to most of the women I've talked to, but I can relate and empathize. I'm going to take a training course at Bellevue starting in March to prepare for a paid position at Sanctuary for Families. I'm still too weak from the operation to train now, but by then, I'll be ready."

"What about your degree?"

"I have to put that off for the moment."

"Dare I ask if your numbness is dissipating?"

"I'm coming along." Changing the uncomfortable subject, Zelda asked, "When are you going to tell me who's coming for dinner?"

Grace knew when she was defeated. "The big surprise is Lulu and Roger. I'd called Georgia Weld inviting her and Doug, and she said she'd just gotten word from Lulu saying she and Roger would be arriving from Israel. So all four of them are coming. Plus you, me, Jeremy and Eliza."

"Oh my God, the Feldmans! I'm so excited they're coming! You know they're scheduled to move back here permanently in August. Not certain exactly where yet but in the New York area." Doing the count on her fingers, she said, "Wait, that's only eight."

"Ann and Eli are coming to stay here for a few days."

After a moment, Zelda asked, "Does Eli know I'm staying overnight?"

"He does."

Zelda paused and let that sink in.

"He's crazy about you, Zelda. Surely, you must know."

"Did he say that to you directly?"

"He didn't have to. I can tell."

"You could be wrong, you know."

"Highly unlikely." Grace got up to stoke the fire.

Just then, Jeremy burst in, arctic air radiating from his clothing. He stripped off his parka, scarf and gloves and joined them around the fire. After greeting Jeremy warmly, Zelda asked for his opinion on Grace's new look.

"I told her she's a vain and extravagant old trout, and she told me sisters are a rare and precious commodity. Upon reflection, I think she's right, so I'm keeping her, no matter what she looks like." His old tabby cat jumped onto his lap. "A wise man once told me women and cats do as they please, so men and dogs just better get used to it."

Sensing the time had come for the evening to end, Zelda said goodnight and climbed the stairs. Before getting into bed, she cracked the window a bit then burrowed under the covers, pulling them up over her ears. She let her mind drift towards Eli and had to admit she was content knowing he'd be arriving tomorrow, content knowing Lulu would be coming, content to be in this cozy house with these unusual twins.

The next day was one of those halcyon winter days with an impossibly blue, cloudless sky. The thermometer showed a bracing fifteen degrees, and though there was little wind, what there was of it wasn't factored in.

Ann called from the road saying she and Eli would arrive around noon. "I'm bringing homemade oyster stew," she said. "I hope we can all have lunch together."

This appeared to be welcome news to Jeremy who told Grace and Zelda that Ann's version tasted even better than the one at Grand Central Station's Oyster Bar.

He rushed out to get salad ingredients and came back with a large box of oyster crackers and two dozen red roses. "We need to cheer this place up," he said. Looking around, he realized he'd already made this purchase. The place was crawling with roses. "I'll just put these in Ann's room. So nice of her to make that stew."

Grace glanced at Zelda before replying, "Red's her favorite color. She'll love them."

"Do you really think she will?" Jeremy turned towards Grace, looking hopeful and helpless with his hands full of flowers.

"Give those to me, and I'll put them in three vases. You can put one by the bed, one in the bathroom and one on the bureau."

"Thank you, Gracie. Please hurry so everything will be ship-shape before she gets here. I'll run get a baguette and a couple of bottles of sparkling cider."

"And get lettuce this time."

Jeremy snapped his fingers. "Knew I forgot something. Be right back."

At noon, Jeremy stood on the front steps of his farmhouse watching the car twist its way through the winter countryside and up the curving driveway. He felt the sting of snowflakes before he could see them slipping from the sky. His first thought was that Ann might like to take a walk in the snow. His second thought was, she'd hate that. Shifting his weight from side to side, he took mental inventory of the games cupboard. They could play Scrabble, backgammon or Monopoly. Or maybe she would prefer to read a book, sitting beside him in front of the fire. Or maybe she would shut herself away in her room for a nap.

The car eased to a standstill. He jumped to open the passenger door.

"By Golly, Ann, I'm glad to see you!"

She turned in her seat and lifted her hand. "I'm so happy to be here!" Grinning from ear to ear, he leaned over and put his hand under her elbow, easing her out of the car and guiding her up the gray gravel path.

# Chapter Twenty-eight

Camaraderie between the older adults covered the tension between Zelda and Eli during lunch. Eli, not wanting to push Zelda, gave the impression of being cold, and Zelda, unsure of herself, felt rejected.

Dinner continued in the same vein. But Georgia Weld and her daughter, Lulu Feldman, managed to keep everyone laughing until the clock finally struck twelve. It was rushed hugs and fast to bed after that.

Zelda took off at eight the next morning before Ann or Eli came downstairs. Hers seemed to be the only car on the Long Island Expressway, underlining her sense of isolation.

Suspecting Eli's disappointment, Grace sat beside him at breakfast. "Cat's got your tongue, dearie?"

"Only tired. What time did Zelda leave?"

"You just missed her. She had to get back to her kids. Moving here has been a big adjustment for them all."

"I invited her to come to Connecticut when the wisteria blooms."

"When's that?"

"May."

"Call her in April." Grace poured more coffee into Eli's cup.

"Seems like a long time from now."

"It's not, Eli. Leave her alone. She's skittish."

"Okay, I get it. Divorce sucks."

"It's more than that. Don't ask. Come to San Francisco for spring break. We can go look for owls."

"I will. I promise."

In late January, Zelda realized she hadn't heard from Brooke in a while and wondered what was happening. Searching for late night solace, she found herself alone in the kitchen and picked up her cell to make the call. Brooke answered right away with a cheery, "Hello," followed by, "Hope you're still planning on being here for the hospital benefit. I put you at my table."

"Sorry, won't be able to make it. My ribs haven't healed yet, and I overdid it a couple of days ago. Now, I'm creeping around like I'm a hundred with doctor's orders to cool it for another six weeks."

"You've got to take better care of yourself."

"Don't worry, my parents are now the ones overdoing it." Zelda sat at the kitchen table with a cup of tea. 'Tell me what you're going to wear."

"Deep, dark secret."

"Well, who's at your table?"

"Grace and her brother, Donna and your brother, Don Peck and whoever he drags in, Ethan Wilder—my TV star—and me. I was counting on you and someone. The heavy hitters are at Stuart's table."

"Don Peck? After all that went down?" Zelda pulled her hair in frustration.

"He's still on Stuart's team."

"I heard a rumor about an SEC investigation."

"Not happening. Time to change the subject."

Zelda poured honey into her tea. "Umm, I'm a devoted fan of *Healing Arts* and will be following the auction of the speaking part with great interest."

"A lot of people want that part."

"I hope you've convinced Stuart it's yours."

"He definitely gets the picture."

After jiggling the tea bag, Zelda yanked it from the cup and dumped it on the saucer. "Is it a one-item auction or do you have other offerings?"

"People want to talk and dance. One big thing like this is enough. Bidding starts at a hundred grand. I'm the auctioneer."

"Wow!"

"The hospital needs the money, and it's tax deductible."

"How high will Stuart go?"

"If he's smart, he'll just keep bidding." Zelda could hear the confidence in Brooke's voice.

"Like I've always said, you're a force of nature."

"Stuart wants the press as much as anyone. I'm sure Silverman will chip in if it gets too wild. I'm hoping it'll go for a million bucks."

"I wish I could be there."

"Me, too," Brooke said. "Stuart is just coming through the door. Got to go. Feel better."

The morning after the benefit, Zelda kept checking her watch until it seemed like a reasonable time to call Grace for gala details. It was ten-thirty, New York time, when her patience came to an end. She shut the door to her room and made herself comfortable in the armchair by the window.

Grace answered right away saying, "I was just about to pick up the phone to call you. Scrambled eggs are sitting in front of Jeremy, and I have a fresh cup of coffee, so I have time to fill you in."

"Tell me about the auction first."

"A lot of testosterone."

"I need more than that." Zelda kicked her shoes off and tucked her legs under her bottom.

"The first part went to Stuart for one million, four hundred thousand."

"Oh my God!"

"Wait for it." Grace paused dramatically. "Then Ethan Wilder, the actor, stood up and announced the show would donate an additional speaking part—Brooke nearly fell over, and I'm sure it was genuine surprise."

"*And*?"

"Eight hundred thousand to Aaron Miller who works with Stuart. Do you know him?"

"Yes, but not well. That's serious money. Brooke must be thrilled."

"She is, and there's a *serious* amount of publicity for her *and* Silverman. It's front-page here today. Last night, it was on the late night news and again this morning."

"Amazing!" Zelda could hear the excitement in her own voice. She leapt out of the chair and started pacing.

"Jeremy says he's sure Silverman will write the whole thing off. Not a penny out of Stuart's or Aaron's pockets."

"I'm not sure how that works. Were the TV crews there during the auction?"

"Of course. Everyone said San Francisco has never seen anything like it."

"That's Brooke. Anything else I should know?"

"Eli and Ann came at the last minute."

"Don't tell me—you talked Eli's ear off, and Jeremy cozied up to Ann."

"Right, and I'd say Hank and Donna are definitely an item."

"Not news," Zelda said. "What about the décor?"

"Very restrained. Zen-like. The food was local, healthy, and delicious. Swanson Vineyards gave the wines, so they were fabulous. Thirty tables of ten at two thousand bucks a head. Jeremy and I had a blast, but I'm certainly glad I didn't have to pay for the tickets."

Restless, Zelda looked out at the empty street. "Did Taylor put false eyelashes on you?"

"They were magnificent and are still hanging on. How long do they last?"

"A few days. Take a selfie and send it to me. What did Brooke wear?"

"She looked like a really rich nurse. She had on a sexy white satin backless number and a 1930s style nurses' hat with whopping diamond earrings dangling down practically to her shoulders. Oh, yes, and a red sequined stethoscope around her neck."

"Not nurses' shoes, I would imagine."

"Definitely not nurses' shoes, but very flattering to her endless legs."

"Any swag?"

"Discreet boxes of Ghirardelli chocolates for everyone."

"Just right. I'll give her another couple of hours to sleep, and then I'll call and congratulate her."

Once Zelda got Brooke on the phone, she couldn't get her off. ABC had contacted her to be on the local morning show, and Jimmy Kimmel's assistant had called wanting her to come to LA and be his guest within the week. This news came with an exhaustive discussion of fashion options.

Brooke couldn't resist boasting. "The Silverman brass from New York called at the crack of dawn to congratulate me on the publicity. They're going to pick up the whole tab. And I can have the sacrosanct company apartment in the Pierre Hotel when I go to New York to tape *Healing Arts* no matter how long it takes."

"You're on a roll!"

"You bet I am, and Liane says I have Jupiter ascending, so this will be a long period of good fortune."

"Does she do Stuart's chart, too?"

"Of course, and we're in perfect sync. I've got to go. It's Raj Methay. See you in New York."

That evening, Brooke called Zelda back. "Rebecca Miller doesn't want the part, and I think Silverman's going to give me her time, expanding my part."

"Will that be a problem with SAG-AFTRA?"

"Stuart will insist that all requirements be scrupulously adhered to, I can assure you."

"So what happens now?"

"The show writers write me in, and off I go to the Big Apple. I hope taping takes forever. I love New York."

"Can I come watch?"

"I'll find out. Anyway, why don't you spend a couple of nights in the apartment with me? We could go to a Broadway show. What haven't you seen?"

"I haven't seen anything. Strict budget these days."

"I thought the house sold."

"It did. Long story."

"Maybe Stuart will bring Taylor and Audrey for a weekend. He's hoping I can get on one of the morning shows in New York."

"I bet you can."

With a stab at modesty, Brooke said, "Maybe they won't want me." Zelda could almost hear her lowering her eyelids and smiling her secret smile.

As it turned out, they did want her. They all wanted her.

# Chapter Twenty-nine

Silverman had had quite a bit of negative publicity recently, so to have the lovely Brooke Duncan splashed around in connection with saving a hospital in San Francisco was just the benediction needed to polish their image. Of course, nobody thought she'd really saved it, but two and a half million dollars was raised—a healthy injection by any standards—and her presentation was sensational. Silverman executives were encouraged to use their media influence to give her maximum coverage while she was in New York.

Their contacts were powerful, and Brooke's photograph was prominent on Page Six even before she arrived in late March. She was booked on talk shows, morning, evening and late, late. Interviewers trailed her to the tapings of *Healing Arts* and tagged along when she went shopping with Zelda. She was offered tickets to many Broadway productions and access to the showrooms of the most coveted designers.

Silverman wanted to keep this salubrious phenomenon going as long as possible and arranged for Brooke's minor role in the TV series to continue for six weeks. During the course of her celebrity status, Brooke began to forget her part on *Healing Arts* was bought and paid for by Silverman and began to think the interviewers were interested in her acting career, rather than her expertise in raising money.

As one interviewer pointed out, her brilliance was in arranging for Silverman to put their PR budget into the hospital. Brooke hadn't thought of it that way and looked thoroughly confused for a moment before flashing a knowing smile and nodding. The truth of the matter was, Brooke's greatest asset was being remarkably photogenic. No one really cared that she was an untalented actor, and the talk show hosts continued to invite her.

Although Zelda was doing her training at Bellevue most days, Brooke asked her to go to several plays. But these plans were always cancelled at the last minute with Brooke explaining it was crucial for her career to take this make-up artist or that important PA or someone's chauffeur instead of Zelda.

Zelda took her hurt feelings to Grace. Always conscious of the time change, she waited 'til noon and called from her childhood bedroom.

"This is the fourth time Brooke's ditched me in favor of someone she only met a few minutes ago. I *never* get to Broadway, and I *really* wanted to see that play."

"Brooke's enjoying her fifteen minutes of fame. Don't take it personally."

"Of course I take it personally. I am the *person* she invited two weeks ago."

"Listen, dearie, there's nothing you can do, so don't waste your indignation. Save it for something more interesting."

"I did get to go with her to a couple of Seventh Avenue showrooms. One of them actually had models parading around in clothes they thought Brooke would like."

"There you go. *I'd* be delighted to take you to the theatre, but I could never get you into couture houses."

"Hardly couture houses but a first for me, anyway."

"Have you been to the company suite at the Pierre yet?"

"I was disappointed. Blue damask and mahogany furniture. Very nice but no character."

"Due to the nature of its use, bland and expensive-looking is all that's required."

"Yeah, but still...Brooks seems to like it well enough. They're going to have a hard time getting her out. She's been photographed at Silverman Midtown. That's where Nick works. She said she didn't see him, though."

"Do you think about him a lot?"

"I *talk* about him a lot—to the lawyer, to the children, to my parents. Other than that, not much thinking."

"What about you? Have you finished your training at Bellevue?"

"End of May. Then I go from volunteer to paid at Sanctuary for Families. I know it's what I'm meant to do."

"A high calling, and unfortunately, you have empirical experience to share."

The next day, Zelda closed her bedroom door and phoned Grace again. "Eli left a voicemail for me this morning saying the wisteria is budding up. He said I should come with the kids on Memorial Day weekend."

"Well?"

"Brooke will be gone by then."

"What has Brooke got to do with this?"

"Nothing," Zelda admitted.

"Well?'

"I'm going to call him back and accept. Have you seen him lately?"

"He was here for ten days in March."

"Did he ask about me?"

"You're both friends of mine, and I'd like it to remain that way by keeping all conversations confidential."

Zelda could feel blood rushing to her face. "Of course, you're right. I'm sorry."

"No need to be sorry, just understand."

"How's Ann?"

"She and Jeremy have gone to Florida—Hobe Sound—where we all first met so many years ago."

"You should've gone with them."

"I wasn't invited."

"Interesting!"

"I think so, too. They're coming back next week. I'll keep you posted."

Zelda's days were filled with family, her Bellevue training and new job, divorce lawyers and occasional forays into fashion with Brooke. Before she knew it, it was time to pack and go to Eli's for the weekend. At the last minute, she decided to leave the twins with one of her sisters.

She rented a sedan, buckled Phoebe and Chloe into the backseat and turned on Google maps. Two hours later, they turned left into Blendon Farm's entrance gate and drove through a wooded area alive with wildflowers. Soon the lovely old stone house came into view. The road forked and Zelda could see Eli's barn off to the right. She hesitated but chose the main house.

A wide, heavy wooden door stood open with the screen door slightly ajar. Zelda rang the bell while Phoebe and Chloe skipped around the car. Ann appeared almost instantly with open arms to welcome them into a classically beautiful square front hall. Behind her, Zelda could see Jeremy, his Coke-bottle wire-rims glinting cheerfully in the afternoon sun.

"Girls, girls come and give us hugs!" Ann embraced each in turn, then turned to Jeremy. "Can you help Zelda with the bags, while I get the lemonade going and call Eli?"

"Your wish is my command, ladies," Jeremy said and winked at Phoebe and Chloe.

"Zelda, you and the girls will stay in the barn, and Eli's coming here to chaperone Jeremy and me. How was the drive? Did you have any trouble finding us?"

"Easy trip. What can I do to help?"

"Go with Jeremy and put your things in the guestrooms, then come back here. Leave the girls with me."

Jeremy got into the passenger seat, and when they arrived at the barn, Eli was waiting for them. Somehow, Jeremy's presence dispelled whatever awkwardness there might have been between Zelda and Eli. They fell into comfortable banter, and once the bags were taken care of, the three of them walked slowly back to the main house, leaving Zelda's rental at the barn.

They found the girls in the kitchen with Ann, and as they walked in, Ann said, "Eli will show you around. I'm commandeering Jeremy for the second nine. We broke for lunch."

Eli said, "Mom never sits still in the daytime. Poor Jeremy has played more golf in the last six months than in his whole life to date."

Jeremy smiled, jingling the change in his pocket. "I'm not complaining. I won fifty-cents this morning."

"I'll get that back," Ann said and walked out the door, calling over her shoulder, "You're on your own for dinner. We're going to the Deens."

Eli put his fingers to his mouth and whistled. "Come on, kids, it's time for the garden tour. There's a gazebo and a maze. Have you ever seen a maze?"

"You mean like in a puzzle book?" Phoebe asked.

"Like that but with a hedge taller than I am outlining it."

The little girls wriggled with delight and left several chocolate chip cookies uneaten. As they were walking through the hall, Zelda looked closely at the walls. "How unusual. At first I thought it was white."

"Mom always tells people the color is called Elephant's Breath. She probably made that up, but it's good, don't you think?"

"Love it."

They continued out to the terrace. Zelda gasped. "Elephant's Breath with wisteria! It's the ideal combination."

"Come *on*, Mom. The maze." Seven-year-old Phoebe had to be stern with her mother at times, just to keep her on track.

They moved towards the door. Shepherding them out into the garden and towards the maze, Eli gently prodded them, like a conscientious sheep dog. "I thought we'd have dinner under the wisteria tonight. Spaghetti. What time do the girls eat?"

Zelda looked at her watch. It was four. "How about six-thirty?"

"Fine. Now tell me a little about your job. I don't know what you do."

"I'm a domestic violence advocate. That means I counsel women who have been abused and take them to various agencies, like courts, medical insurance offices, legal counseling. I escort them to job training sessions and help find suitable housing."

"What got you interested in this?"

*OMG, of course, he doesn't know* flashed through Zelda's mind. She was speechless for a moment and, thinking fast, said nonchalantly, "Oh, you know, my family's in law enforcement, so I've heard a lot. The women need practical help more than therapy, and I help them establish an independent life."

"Where did you train?"

"Bellevue. Nothing but the best."

They came to the mouth of the maze, the girls shivering with excitement. Eli said, "My mother would tell you this labyrinth is laid out on ley lines and there's a vortex in the center, whatever that means. I'll go first this time, but tomorrow you can go on your own. Follow closely now, and don't get lost."

Eli stepped onto the fragrant cedar chip path, stopped and dramatically held up his hand for silence. "Make a worthy wish and dwell on it as we wander the wonderful way to the vortex of wishes-come-true." Giggling, they followed. He had forgotten there was a decorative wellhead in the center, and he was unprepared—no coins to throw in. "Never mind," he said. "I'll have plenty of pennies for you tomorrow."

# Chapter Thirty

E ven though it was still daylight when they sat down for dinner, Eli placed candles on the table. The heavenly scent of wisteria became more pronounced as the heat of the day relented. The papery lavender blossoms hung motionless in the stillness, and an orchestra of crickets began tuning up for their summer concerts. All was right with the world.

The little girls were ravenous and tucked into the spaghetti with gusto but let the salad languish in the bowl. A spirited game of *I Spy* ensued despite the fast-falling twilight. By the time the dessert dishes were cleared, it was dark enough to see a few fireflies signaling to their mates, and there was a hint of chill in the air.

Soon, it was off to the barn for the Blairs. Eli went with them and helped settle the girls down for the night. Afterwards, Zelda relaxed on a deep sofa in the large room facing the stone chimney of a huge fireplace and watched as Eli carefully laid and lit a fire. He came and sat close to her, stretching his arm on the sofa behind her. Alarm bells went off inside Zelda, and she could feel her breath coming fast.

Headlights brushed them as a car turned toward the main house. Ann and Jeremy were back from the Deens. Tension melted out of Zelda's shoulders.

Eli broke the silence. "I plan to take the girls fishing on the river tomorrow. Would you like to come with us or would you like a break?" Eli's voice sounded casual, as if he had no idea of the confusion he'd caused.

"Count me in." Zelda controlled her voice.

"Come over to the house when you want breakfast, and we'll head out as soon as we can after that. I'll make some sandwiches in case we decide to make a day of it."

"Sounds perfect."

"I'm going to shove off now. See you in the morning." Eli waved as he closed the door behind him.

Zelda took her disappointment into her bedroom to examine it, leaving the fire to roar at the empty living room.

Is it just Eli, or am I frightened of all men, all intimacy? How can I long for something that repels me? What's wrong with me?

She tried to think about this logically. She tried to think what Shookie would say and what she'd learned at Bellevue. She had no answers, so she picked up her phone and called Grace. "Have I got you at a good time?"

"I'm at home reading papers. Are you at Eli's?"

"Yes, in the barn."

"Utter bliss."

Zelda explained her conflicted feelings as best she could and concluded by saying, "I know I sound like an adolescent, but this is how I feel."

"Nine months ago, you were viciously attacked by your husband of nearly a decade, the father of your four children. You'd been living with these assaults for more than six years, pretending they weren't happening. This is severe denial, Zelda, and you allowed this to go on and on.

"I know you've been talking to Shookie for almost a year now, and I'm sure you learned a lot at Bellevue, but you've got to acknowledge you had a part in this. Looking the other way is like consenting to the violence. And until you come to terms with that, you will not be able to move on to another relationship.

"I am very fond you, and Eli is like family to me. I want both of you to be healthy and happy, but I don't see this happening. I see you still stuck in denial, still numb. Please do the healing work you need to do so you can have a mature, loving relationship with a healthy man.

"Forgive me if I sound harsh, but I don't like to see you stringing Eli along."

"Sorry, Grace, you're right. I've only been thinking of myself."

"Time to move on, dearie. You're a smart girl, and you have every tool to help yourself."

"I'll call you next week." Wounded and sulky, Zelda went into the living room and gazed at the fire, allowing it to lull her with its hypnotic dance. Eventually feeling calm, she went to bed, and when she woke, most of her anti-Grace feelings were gone. She even admitted to herself there was work to be done.

When Eli's family bought Blendon Farm, there had been a rickety dock with a tumbled down boathouse on the property. Eli's father fixed them up, and bought a 1950s wooden boat loaded with bright work, only twenty feet in length but very beamy. The perfect boat for today's catch and release excursion. Eli didn't know what the original name was as she'd been re-christened *The Ann* when he first knew her. *The Ann* was always referred to as *Than*, and she was ready and waiting by the time the girls finished breakfast.

The weather was overcast, but warm, and the fish were jumping. They stayed on the river until suppertime and arrived back to find Jeremy's hamburgers and corn on the cob already on the grill.

After getting the girls into bed, Eli again laid and lit the fire, but this time, Zelda was standing behind him. When he stood, he took her in his arms. She shoved him away, roughly, and then tried to pull him back. "There are things you don't know about me, Eli, and I have to make some changes before I can have any kind of relationship."

The look on his face made her add, " But I don't want to lose you."

"Then, don't, Zelda," he said as he headed out the door.

The next morning when Zelda and the girls arrived at the house for breakfast, Ann said, "The principal of Eli's school called early this morning, and even though it's Memorial Day, he was needed at the office. I expect he'll be back by lunchtime. Come on in and have some pancakes."

"That sounds great, but we'll have to leave after breakfast. The traffic is going to be terrible, and the girls have school tomorrow."

"Eli will be disappointed, but I'm sure he'll understand."

Zelda brooded all day Monday and Tuesday, but on Wednesday morning, she called Dr. Mary Zachary, who'd been her mentor at Bellevue. They met after work at Moonstruck, a diner in the hospital. After three cups of tea and floods of Zelda's tears, Mary suggested EMDR—Eye Movement Desensitization and Reprocessing—psychotherapy for Zelda. Clearly, she needed to try something different, and Mary managed to schedule sessions compatible with Zelda's working hours.

Eli didn't call after the weekend, and even though Zelda got over being annoyed at Grace and started calling her again, she never asked about Eli. Grace never volunteered news about Eli or Ann.

Within a month, it was evident that Zelda was responding to EMDR therapy. She felt better, more centered, but Eli became the new elephant in the living room.

Summer turned into autumn, and the kids settled into their schools. They saw Nick occasionally and seemed to have no problem accepting life as it was, living with their mother in their grandparent's home. Other kids in their classes had similar situations. The Blair children had the added benefit of dozens of cousins and Kevin with his awe-inspiring security detail, always impressive to school friends. Abigail had the right touch, and the house was filled with children, games, laughter.

Zelda's divorce would be final in November. Not feeling up to taking college courses in the fall semester, she sought something outside of family and work to engage her mind.

In mid-September, she dressed carefully and went by subway to a famous bridge club in Midtown Manhattan. She was astonished to run into Dr. Mary there. They had both enrolled in the beginner class, which was scheduled every Tuesday evening at six forty-five for the next three months.

Soon they started getting together with other novice players once a week, and as they both had good card sense, they made a winning team. With friendship burgeoning, Mary started joining in on family bowling and pizza nights, and occasionally, Sunday lunches at the O'Neils.

Roger Feldman applied for and was accepted by a synagogue in Scarsdale and Lulu and he moved back to the States. Even though it was only forty miles to Zelda's, neither she nor Lulu had had a moment in the past two months to make the short trip. Zelda's life was overflowing, and Lulu had the whole congregation to discover. Lulu was finding being a rabbi's wife was a full-time job.

On a crisp and sunny Saturday in October, Mary picked up Zelda and the kids in her battered SUV, and they made their way to the Bronx Zoo to meet up with Lulu.

"Oh my God, Zelda, you didn't tell me Mary looks like Scarlett Johansson." Lulu hugged the children and Zelda, blowing a kiss to Mary at the same time.

Stepping back and looking at Mary closely, Zelda said, "Oh my God, she really does! How'd I miss that?"

"With your head in the clouds, as usual. Mary, it's really nice to have you as part of the zoo."

Mary laughed and said, "I've always been part of a zoo. This one's just bigger and better than most."

The three women enjoyed themselves as much as the children, and the day ended late in the afternoon with Lulu threatening to join the bridge class. "I know I'm coming in the middle, but I'm *much* better than Zelda at math. I'll catch up fast."

# Chapter Thirty-one

A few days later, Zelda had only just arrived at her office when her cell rang. Seeing it was her lawyer, she closed the door before answering.

He was not a man to beat around the bush. "I have a decree nisi regarding your divorce on my desk. As long as there are no unforeseen circumstances, your divorce will be final within six weeks."

"What kind of circumstances would that be?"

"Don't worry. Not a chance Nick will try to block it."

"Is there anything I need to do?"

"Everything's handled by the court. I'll keep in touch. Any second thoughts?"

Zelda paused long enough for him to say, "Zelda?"

"No second thoughts."

Without plans for the evening and wanting to avoid discussing her feelings with her parents, she called Mary. "Can we have an early dinner together?"

"I was going to Zumba, but I can cancel if it's important."

Again, Zelda hesitated, and Mary said, "I'll meet you at Moonstruck. Six-thirty."

"How about some other place?"

"Okay. Riverpark."

"Oh, good! I'll make the reservation. My treat."

Once the two women were comfortably seated and their order had been placed, Mary could contain her curiosity no longer. "So. What's up?"

"My divorce will be final in less than six weeks."

"How does that make you feel?"

"Relieved, anxious, lonely, sad and glad."

"Sounds about right."

"I'm not crazy?"

"Of course not. But don't you dare romanticize the marriage and relapse back into denial. You were in a dangerous situation."

"I know. And I know my parents aren't upset that I'm the first to divorce in the family. It's just me. I feel guilty."

"Feelings aren't facts, Zelda. Go ahead and feel relieved, anxious, lonely, sad, glad *and* guilty, but know, intellectually, you're doing the right thing."

Zelda nodded her head. "Let's eat fast and go see if we can pick up a bridge game at the club."

"As a doctor, I'd say it's healthy for you to sit with these feelings, but as your friend, I'd say you can't romanticize and count to thirteen at the same time. So let's go."

They scarfed down their dinner and headed for the club.

The day of the divorce was an anti-climax. The lawyer called and told Zelda it was over. She was free. It happened on her day off, and wanting to participate somehow, Zelda asked him not to mail the document. She told him she'd rather pick it up at his office. It was waiting for her at the reception desk.

She left the building feeling down. Hunching her shoulders against the wind, she looked up at the threatening sky and walked east, towards Bellevue, calling Mary as she went. They planned to meet at Moonstruck in half an hour.

Though the diner wasn't Zelda's favorite, it was convenient for Mary, and Zelda needed to see her. They sat in a booth, and Zelda got right down to business. "After all the divorce proceedings, picking up this thin envelope without even, 'Goodbye and good luck' from my attorney was kind of depressing."

"Divorce is depressing all 'round. Have a little more caffeine and sugar. Some days call for extra poison."

"What am I supposed to do with this?" Zelda held up a plain nine by twelve envelope.

"Put it in your safety deposit box."

"I don't have one."

"Put it with your stock certificates."

"I don't have any."

"Well, put it in the bottom of your underwear drawer and forget about it. But don't lose it. You'll need it when you get married again."

"Married again?" Zelda shivered. "I don't think so."

"Things don't ever turn out the way you expect them to."

"I never told you about Eli Russell. He's a good man, but I drove him off." Zelda held the coffee cup with both hands, as if to warm them.

Mary glanced at her watch. "I want to hear about him, but I've got to get back to work. After bridge tonight, we can go to Starbucks." Scooting out of the booth, she grabbed the check and patted Zelda on the back. "See you at the lesson."

It was only eleven-thirty, and the day stretched ahead of Zelda like a desert. Her parents were working, her kids at school, Lulu in Scarsdale. Pulling out her phone, she called Hank. The moment his voicemail came on, she remembered he'd be in court all day.

She gestured for the waitress, who said, "Just so you know, Dr. Z paid for an extra cup of coffee. She said you'd need it."

"I guess today's my lucky day. Thanks."

While drinking her coffee, Zelda scrolled through her contacts and made a few calls hoping to find someone free for lunch. Unsuccessful. It was eight-thirty in California, so she tried Grace. Voicemail. Reluctantly, she shoved her arms into her coat and made for the door. To chase away the blues, she decided she'd stay in Manhattan, take in the holiday decorations and do some shopping. Resolute, she lifted her yellow umbrella and stepped out of fluorescent lighting and into cascading sleet, which was icing the city with its gritty varnish.

Thirty minutes later she was examining one of Saks Fifth Avenue's side windows with her back to St. Patrick's Cathedral. Out of nowhere, searing pain shot through her torso. Zelda fell forward, her head smashing against the plate glass. Still conscious, she collapsed on the pavement.

Though she couldn't see it, she could smell blood running down her face and could hear someone yelling, "Police!" Kick after vicious kick bounced her limp body along the sidewalk. The pain engulfed her. She slipped into shock, her cheerful umbrella lying broken at her side. Sleet pelted down.

A crowd had gathered, and some were taping the incident on iphones, recording two powerful young men pulling Nick away from Zelda's motionless form. One woman approached Zelda, but then, a man said, "Wait for the medics. Could be spinal injuries."

High-pitched wails of emergency vehicles reached through her semi-consciousness and brought her back. She wanted to move, but found she could not. Sensing the space around her was clear, she perceived a man in blue kneeling down beside her, her driver's license in his hand. "Good God. She's the Commissioner's daughter," he said. "Radio headquarters."

Someone slipped an oxygen mask on; someone moved her gently. Was that Nick in handcuffs? She tried hard to stay with them but slid into darkness.

Zelda came to in the intensive care unit with a full complement of tubes and drips. Her parents were there, and a sprinkling of siblings were standing around the bed. Despite the tube down her throat, she tried to speak, but was only able to produce a feeble humming noise.

"You're safe at Lenox Hill Hospital," her father said evenly.

Closing her eyes, Zelda tried to focus her mind on what had happened. The hammering pain in her head clouded her thoughts, and despite the morphine, the pains in her chest and back collided in explosive agony.

Abigail took her hand and sat on the side of the bed. No one spoke for a few minutes, and then Kevin's soothing voice recounted some of the details, ending with, "Nick's in custody. Nothing for you to worry about."

How much of this information got through to Zelda was unclear, but Abigail thought she felt weak pressure on her hand. Perhaps it signaled Zelda had understood.

A nurse arrived and shooed the siblings out. Only Kevin and Abigail stayed. Zelda was still in danger.

By this time it was nearly eight o'clock, and Kevin said to Abigail, "Go have dinner. I'll stay here. Why don't you call Grace? She's been such a good friend."

Abigail was not interested in eating but found a quiet corner to make the call. Seeing the screen, Grace answered. "Abigail! I was just about to call Zelda back. I arrive two weeks from today."

"Grace, Zelda's in intensive care. Nick spotted her on the street—she was only window shopping—and he...attacked." Abigail's voice was shaky.

"I'll come today, if you need me."

"There is nothing you can do. She has cerebral hemorrhaging, cardiac contusions, a cracked sternum, broken nose, several fractured vertebrae, a lacerated liver and damage to one of her kidneys. The liver may require surgery. Obviously no visitors."

"Oh my poor darling Zelda! What have they done with Nick?"

"He's in the holding pen. Midtown North. I'm sure he'll plead temporary insanity—today was the day the divorce was final—but there's no way Kevin will let him get away with that."

"Do the kids know?"

"Not yet. On second thought, Grace, please come. Stay with us. The children adore you. It would be great for all of us to have you here."

"I can still make the red-eye. I'll be there in the morning."

Abigail could feel some of the pressure in her neck ease up. "Take a taxi to our house. Someone will be there to let you in. I'm so glad you're coming."

As Abigail cut the connection, she saw Mary walking towards her, and said, "You'll need to sweet-talk the nurses into letting you into the ICU, and I'm not sure if Zelda would even realize you're there."

"Don't worry. They'll let me see her. I'll stay the night. You look like you could use some rest."

"I couldn't."

"Look, Abigail, I'm used to sleeping in hospital chairs, and I'm off tomorrow. Go home."

"Kevin's in there."

"He can go home with you."

Mary and Kevin stayed the night.

# Chapter Thirty-two

S till shattered inside and out, Zelda rolled out of the hospital in a power wheelchair five weeks after the assault. Against medical advice, she went straight home with a nurse's aide, instead of going to the recommended rehab facility, and although she hadn't needed liver surgery, her recovery was slow.

The highlights of her convalescent weeks were one-way telephone calls from Grace. Being too weak for conversation, Zelda would put her phone on speaker, prop herself up on a pile of pillows and take in Grace's news with great interest, relieved not having to muster any sort of response.

During these calls Zelda followed the fizzle of the Donna-Hank relationship. Apparently, those bi-coastal romantics didn't have enough in common to triumph over time and distance. Meanwhile, Brooke had met someone in New York, a man senior to Stuart in every way, older, more powerful and a man who was determined to see Stuart's star wane. They solved the bi-coastal problem with Brooke opening a New York chapter of her life. Grace predicted a Duncan divorce and wedding bells for Brooke. She also told Zelda she suspected the Ann-Jeremy romance was heating up and regretted she was thousands of miles away, unable to confirm her suspicions.

Other pleasures for Zelda were the bouquets and cheery notes that Eli sent regularly. She was touched that he never let a holiday pass unobserved, always including each child by sending cards and thoughtful packages.

It turned out Grace was right about Ann and Jeremy, and a wedding was being planned at Blendon Farm at the end of May. Zelda still required help bathing and putting on her back brace, but nothing would stop her from going to the wedding. So with her nurse's aide at the wheel of a rental car, she set out for Blendon Farm.

It was exactly one year since her last visit, and she thought sadly of that time she'd run away from her confused feelings about Eli then and left so much unsaid. Even though he'd faithfully kept in touch, she hadn't seen him for an entire year. Would she feel awkward around him this weekend? She wondered.

Grace would be there when she arrived and would share the barn with her and the nurse. Zelda had still been in the hospital the last time she'd seen Grace. It would be wonderful to be with her again, Zelda thought. She smiled remembering the weekly phone calls and how much Grace's friendship had helped her endure and start to heal.

As the nurse drove her through the countryside towards Connecticut, Zelda's thoughts turned to Brooke. At the end of the two and a half hour trip from Long Island they came to the end of the driveway, and Zelda's spirits soared seeing Grace standing in front of the barn waving them over. They fell into each other's arms, and Zelda's nurse had to remind her of her promise to take it easy. Eventually, the nurse prevailed and tucked Zelda into bed. Having arrived the day before, Grace was ready with a plate of sandwiches. She plunked herself down on a chair at the foot of the bed facing Zelda.

"Go ahead, Zelda. I can tell you are full of questions." Grace bit into a tuna sandwich.

"Tell me more about Brooke. She called me a few times, but the calls were always hurried or interrupted."

"Her marriage is over. Stuart is staying in San Francisco, and she has moved to New York. Taylor is going to Northwestern in the fall, and Audrey will finish high school in San Francisco, living with Stuart."

"Who's the new man?"

"I really don't know, Zelda. All I know is, he's a very big deal at Silverman."

"I've got to call her."

"Do you feel up to talking about Nick?"

Zelda heaved a deep sigh. "Not really, but I'll give you the Cliff Notes. His diagnosis is psychopathic personality with anger control disorder. He pled temporary insanity but was convicted of attempted homicide and is serving fourteen to twenty in Attica."

"How are the kids handling all this?" Opening a Coke for each, Grace put Zelda's on the bedside table.

"My father has been incredible. He's spending a lot of time with them, playing games, taking trips, involving them in community service. Makes such a difference, but of course, there are many hurdles."

"And you, dearie?" Grace passed the potato chips to Zelda.

"Post-traumatic stress therapy for me and some family group sessions. And I'm continuing with the EMDR."

"EMDR?"

"The eye movement thing."

"Oh, right. Well, any light at the end of the tunnel?"

"Definitely. I remind myself every day that I have four great kids and need one hundred percent recovery. Very motivating. I don't have the luxury of wallowing around in denial anymore. Finally accepted that." Zelda swung her legs to the floor and pulled on her sneakers. "Let's go for a walk."

She leaned heavily on her walking stick but could keep a good pace. "Let's walk to the labyrinth or maze or whatever it is."

They passed the pergola laden with wisteria and wandered through the lovely garden out to the maze. The hedges had grown, and the women were completely invisible from outside as they made their way over the cedar chips to the well in the center. Zelda reached into her pocket and brought out a coin. She lifted it dramatically and paused. Closing her eyes, she thought, if only I can have a second chance at life, at love. She threw the coin into the well and said, "I made my wish. How about you?" She offered a dime to Grace.

"Making wishes is my favorite thing, but I like to make at least three at a time. Got any more money in that pocket?"

Zelda held out a handful of change. "Very good," Grace said. "I'll take five. Never like leaving anything to chance." Grace tossed the coins in, one right after the other, as if she'd known all along what her wishes would be.

After making a few wrong turns leaving the maze, they came out into the garden again, and there was Eli. Both women noticed he was looking pale with dark circles under his eyes. He hugged them and asked, "How about tea on the porch? I happen to know there are some freshly baked oatmeal cookies in the kitchen."

Zelda felt the tingle in her stomach, which she'd felt so long ago when they'd first met. It seemed natural to take his arm as the three of them walked towards the house.

That night, the local inn was the scene of the bridal dinner. Only twelve people in a small room off the main dining room. The flowers had been arranged by the town's florist, but they had all come from Ann's garden. Masses of pink peonies, pastel sweet peas and roses of many shapes and hues. There were even a few cornflowers and blue-eyed daisies with spikes of white astilbe and pale blue delphinium.

The wedding would be under the awning of wisteria—so no cut flowers needed—and these flowers would come back to Blendon the next day to decorate the dining room.

The evening went on too long for Zelda. She left with her nurse before dessert was served and was fast asleep before Grace crept into the barn a little after midnight.

Having slept soundly, Zelda awoke at five the following morning. She dressed without the back brace and slipped out of the barn just as the eastern horizon was flaunting the promise of dawn. The air, though still, clung to a slight chill. Birds were beginning to awake, and the sky was quickly turning from deep violet to mauve. Zelda stood motionless and listened intently. Sensing the moment was sacred, she reckoned adding the sound of gravel underfoot would be insulting to nature's sunrise symphony.

She noticed a shadow moving from the house coming towards her. It took a few seconds before she recognized Eli. He moved with purpose, rapidly and silently across the lawn.

She leaned on her walking stick and waited.

Eli stepped in front of her and spoke in a rush as if the words were being released under great pressure, like champagne spilling out from where it had been suppressed for years.

"Zelda, I will never find a perfect time for this. So I'm going to tell you something, and I don't want a response today. You can answer tomorrow or ten years from now, it doesn't matter to me."

Eli took a deep breath and continued rapidly. "I want to marry you. I feel like I've been waiting my whole life for you. I know I'm springing this on you without warning, but I couldn't keep it inside any longer. I *love* you. Now that you know how I feel, and will always feel, I can wait for your answer for as long as it takes."

At that moment the lights in Ann's bedroom on the second floor of the main house snapped on. Her face appeared at the window, alert and watchful.

"Mom, it's me." Eli waved his arm.

"Well, stop talking to yourself and get up here and make yourself useful."

Eli turned to Zelda. In his hand was a sprig of wisteria. Putting both his hands on her shoulders, he kissed her tenderly, tucking the lavender blossoms behind her ear. Other lights flickered on in the main house and headlights were coming up the drive. The wedding day was underway. Eli strode to the house, disappearing from Zelda's view.

Shocked, Zelda made her way to the center of the labyrinth where she hurled her walking stick to the ground and flung her arms in the air. "Yes!" she whispered as she twirled around the wellhead. Filled to the brim with happiness, she wanted to throw her arms around the whole wide world.

Faintly, through the thick hedge, she could hear her nurse calling. Leaving her stick where it lay, she wound her way out of the maze on a cloud of joy.

## THE END

# About the Author

Jane Foster was born below sea level in New Orleans. She grew up there with a taste for delicious food and friendly people, and then life took her to New York for thirty-three years. There she studied English literature and art history at Finch College, and after graduating with honors, she worked at Sotheby's as assistant to Chairman John Marion. Later she worked with the famed jeweler, Fred Leighton, and then opened her own jewelry design business. She is a passionate horticulturist, and two of her gardens are included in the Smithsonian Archives of American Gardens. After moving to Florida, Jane served on the board of the Hanley Center, an alcoholism and substance abuse treatment center for nearly two decades. In 2018, she won the Jessica Cosgrave Award for lifetime achievement from Finch College.

Jane has three children, and currently enjoys the best of all worlds, dividing her time between Florida and France.

Jane has written four other novels. Her first novel, Below Sea Level, published in 2013, won an Illumination Book

Award. Her second novel, Sliding, was a finalist for the Eric Hoffer Award. Her third novel, Boulevard Beauséjour, written with Anne Yelland, was nominated for the Book Excellence Award. Her last novel, Careless, published in 2019, also won the Book Excellence Award.